Mara L. Pratt

Legends of Norseland

Mara L. Pratt

Legends of Norseland

ISBN/EAN: 9783337391751

Printed in Europe, USA, Canada, Australia, Japan

Cover: Foto ©Andreas Hilbeck / pixelio.de

More available books at **www.hansebooks.com**

LEGENDS

OF

NORSELAND.

EDITED BY

MARA L. PRATT,

Author of " American History Stories," etc.

Illustrated by A. CHASE

EDUCATIONAL PUBLISHING COMPANY.

BOSTON.

NEW YORK.   CHICAGO.

CONTENTS.

LEGENDS

OF

NORSELAND.

I.

In the beginning, when the beautiful and sunny world was first made, there stood, in the very midst of all its beauty, Mt. Ida — a mountain so high, so far away up among the snowy clouds, that its summit was lost in the shining light of the rays of the sun.

At its base, stretching away to the north, the south, the east, and the west, as far as

even the eyes of the gods could reach, lay the
soft, green valleys and the great, broad plain
beyond.   Encircling the whole great plain,
and curling lovingly around in all the little
bends and bays of the distant shore, lay the
deep blue waters; and beyond the waters,
hidden in the distant mists, rose the great
mountains in which the frost giants dwelt.

On the top of Mt. Ida, the gods had built
their shining city, Asgard; and from its golden
gateway to the valley below was stretched the
richly-colored, rainbow bridge, with its wonderful bars of red and yellow and blue, orange
and green, indigo and purple.

And in this shining city, where the gods
dwelt, there was no sorrow, no grief, no pain
of any kind.   Never was the sun's light shut
off by heavy clouds; never did the cruel lightnings flash, nor came their blights upon the

harvest fields; never did the heavy rains fall, nor did the cold winds sweep down upon this shining city.

But alas, there came a time when a shadow fell upon this city that shone so like a golden cloud resting upon the mountain peak. For the Fates, the three cruel sisters, came and took up their abode at the foot of the wonderful tree of Life, whose roots were in the earth, and whose branches, reaching high above the shining city, protected it from the sun's fierce heat and strong white light. And from that time even the gods themselves were no longer free from care and sorrow.

Envy sprang up among the children of the great god, Odin; sickness, and even death, fell upon them; and the frost giants waged war with them,—a war that would never cease in all the ages that were to come, until that day when

the sun's light went out forever, and the dark
reign of Ragnarok fell upon the earth.

It was a beautiful earth that lay stretched
out at the foot of Mt. Ida. The fields were
rich with grain; the trees were loaded with
fruits; the sun shone warm and bright; but there
were no harvesters, no gatherers of the fruit,
no children to run and frolic in the sunshine.

"The fair earth is desolate," said Odin to
himself, as he looked down from his golden
temple. "There should be people there, not
gods and goddesses like us here upon Mt. Ida,
but beings less powerful than we, beings who
can love and enjoy, and whose children shall
fill the earth with their happy voices. And
the care of all these beings shall be mine."

As he spoke, he, the All Father, passed
down the rainbow bridge, out into the rich,
green valley below.

As he passed on beneath the trees, he saw standing together, their branches bending towards each other, a straight, strong Ash and a gentle, graceful Elm.

"From these trees," said Odin to himself, "will I create the Earth people. The man I will name Ask, and the woman, Embla. It is a beautiful, sunny world: they should be very happy in it. How their children shall delight in the broad fields and the sunny slopes! And no harm shall come to them; for I, the All Father, will watch over them in all the ages to come."

II.

YGDRASIL.

At the base of Mt. Ida stood Ygdrasil, the wonderful tree of Life. Never before nor since was there another such a tree. It had never had a beginning; it had never been young.

Not even the oldest man, not even the gods themselves could say, " I remember when this great tree was a tender sapling, I remember when it sent forth its first tiny leaves, and how it rocked, and swayed, and shivered, and bent its timid head as the cold ice king swept over it."

For there had never been a time since the beginning of the world when Ygdrasil had not stood there, tall and strong, one great root reaching down, down through the earth to the home of the dead, another stretching away, no one could tell how far, till it reached the home of the terrible giants, so fierce and cruel, so strong, and withal so wise, that even the gods themselves dreaded them and stood ever in terror of their approach.

And its branches? So broad, so far reaching, so numerous were these, that they spread themselves protectingly over the whole earth, their top-most leaves rustling and whispering together above the golden palace of the gods, far up on the summit of the cloud-hidden Ida.

Nor was this all. Hidden among the dense leaves lived a great white eagle. No one knew whence he came; no one had ever looked upon him; but there he sat, ages upon ages, singing forever the story of the creator of the earth and the wonderful deeds of the gods who dwell in the shining city of Asgard. The leaves of the tree sang sunset songs, and whispered to each other secrets, sometimes sad, sometimes gay, which even the gods, with all their wisdom, could not understand.

At the foot of the tree, away down at the end even of the deepest, farthest root, lay the Well of Wisdom. Its waters were black. Sometimes they were very bitter, and few there were who had the courage and the perseverance to search out the hiding-place of this wonderful spring. Then, too, it was guarded by a grim old giant, Memory, who so loved this well, and so dreaded the approach of man or god to its waters, that he would not allow them even to touch their lips to it, until they had sworn to surrender to him whatever thing was dearest in life to them.

This was a heavy price to pay for wisdom, and few there were who cared to pay it. "Will you give me your children?" "Will you give me your freedom?" "Will you give me your health?" "Will you give me your tongue, your ears, your eyes?" the old giant would ask of the mortals who came to drink of the waters of the Well of Wisdom.

And always, when the mortals heard these questions, they grew pale and trembled with fear. "Go back to your homes," the old giant would thunder, "you desire wisdom it is true; but you are not willing to pay the price for it." Then the mortals would hurry away, their hearts beating with fear, their ears ringing with the thunderous tones of the terrible giant, who, since the earth was made, had sat at the foot of Ygdrasil guarding the secrets from all the world.

ODIN, THE "ALL FATHER."

III.

ODIN AT THE WELL OF WISDOM.

As Odin looked down from his home in Asgard and saw the people he had made from the ash and the elm trees, he sighed to himself and said, "These are my children. It is I who created them. They are innocent and pure and sweet."

"But, alas, how little they know of life. By and by there will come to them danger and sorrow. The Ice King, the cruel tyrant, will breathe upon them, and the harvests will shrivel before their eyes; the rivers will be frozen, the trees will be bare, and there will be no food for them. As the years roll on, little children will come; these children will grow into manhood and womanhood, and other little children will follow. They are but mortals. Sickness and death will be their share; for I could not make them like the gods."

And as Odin thought of all these things his heart grew sad. Almost he wished he had not made these helpless beings from the ash and the elm. He looked down into the sunny valley, where as yet no sorrow nor suffering had come. "Poor children!" he sighed. "What a world of wisdom Odin must possess to protect and guide and teach these earth-people that he has made."

Just then Ask and Embla paused and looked up towards the shining city; for the sigh from Odin's heart had been so deep and long that the leaves of Ygdrasil had rustled, and a faint echo of it had swept even across the valley below.

" What is it that sweeps sometimes across the valley, and moves the trees and the leaves, and so gently fans our cheeks?" asked Embla.

" I often wonder," answered Ask. " It is very pleasant. Perhaps it is a message from the good Odin who made us and who gave us this sunny valley to play in."

Then on they ran, hand in hand, happy children as they were, and in a moment had forgotten all about it.

But Odin had not forgotten. " Frigg,"

said he to his goddess wife, "it is granted to us as gods to possess great wisdom. Still there remain many things we do not know. Below in the valley there have sprung into being a man and a woman. They are like us, Frigg, but they are not very wise. They need our care, even as our own dear Baldur needed our care when he was a very little child. I shall go to the Giant Memory, who guards the Well of Wisdom, and he shall give me a draught from the wonderful water. Then shall I be the all-wise, all-loving All-Father these children of the valley need."

"O, but the price this cruel Giant will ask of you!" sobbed Frigg.

"I would give my life for them," answered Odin tenderly. Then he turned from her, passed down the rainbow bridge to the valley, entered the great black, gaping cave and groped his way along the cold, dark passages that led to the Well of Wisdom.

Three times the sun rose, three times the sun set. Then, just as the earth and the shining Asgard lay bathed in the rich, golden sunset light, Odin came forth again, passed up the rainbow bridge, and entered the great hall of the gods. " It is Odin," cried Frigg.

Yes, it is Odin, the same Odin. But with a face so joyous, so radiant, so happy! For Odin had drank from the Well of Wisdom. The way had been dark; the struggle with the great Giant had been hard. But Odin had conquered; and now the joy that belongs always to the wise was his forevermore.

IV.

ODIN AND THE ALL-WISE GIANT.

Away across the great sea of blue waters that curled about the shores of Midgard, the dwelling place of Odin's earth-children, were the dark, frowning, rock-bound mountains, the castles of the terrible giants whom even the gods feared.

One of these giants, Vafthrudner, was known among them as the All-wise.

"He is our chief. He is wiser even than the gods of Asgard," the giants sometimes would thunder across the wide blue sea. And indeed it was true; for none among the gods had yet been able to answer his questions; nor could they; neither could they ask of him one that he could not answer.

"We will bear the insolence of this giant no longer," said Odin to Frigg. "I will go to him, and the race of giants shall know that at last Wisdom dwells not in Jotunheim but in the golden city of the gods,—the glorious, shining city of Asgard."

"Who comes?" thundered Vafthrudner as Odin approached his mountain peak.

"It is I — a mere traveller. But as I chanced to be journeying through your country, I heard of your wonderful wisdom. In my own country, far away to the west, I too am accounted somewhat wise. Let us test each other and learn which of us is wiser."

"Test each other! Learn which is wiser!" bellowed the great giant, his voice echoing and re-echoing across the sea, until the very walls of the golden hall upon Mt. Ida trembled and the earth-children in the valley below clung to each other in fear.

"Whichever one fails forfeits his life. You know that, I trust," added Vafthrudner with a sneer.

"I know," answered Odin quietly. "But let us begin. Night will come upon us, and I must reach my home while the Sun-god is still above us."

"You will never see your home again; so it matters little whether we begin early or late.

However, tell me, foolish, vain earth-child
that you are, what river is it that flows
between this home of the All-powerful giants
and the home of the gods?"

"The name of that river is Ifing,"
answered Odin. "And I can tell you more
than that. Because it touches upon the shores
of the city of the gods, the Ice King, Njord,
has no power over it. His breath cannot
freeze it. Year after year, Njord tries to
imprison its sparkling waters that you giants
may cross upon its crust and attack the
shining city. But it will never freeze. You
will never cross it. Asgard is forever
safe."

The giant dropped his mighty jaw. His
eyes stared like great suns of fire. His
terrible frame trembled. Down came his club
upon the floor of his great castle.

Again Ask and Embla paled with fear as the valley shook beneath their feet.

"Who are you?" roared the All-wise giant. "Who are you that you know that river's name? Who are you that you dare tell me I shall never cross to its farther shore?"

"It matters little who I am," answered Odin, his eyes flashing, his beautiful figure growing taller and taller. "But listen now while I whisper into your ear my question." And with a mighty stride Odin crossed to Vafthrudner's throne, leaned forward, seized him by the shoulder, and hissed three words into the gigantic, cave-like ear.

What those words were, no man ever knew. Forever they shall remain a secret between Vafthrudner and the All-Father Odin.

The giant paled, staggered to his feet,

groaned and fell. The walls of the great hall swayed to and fro. The lightning flashed, the thunder pealed from peak to peak. Odin had conquered. The All-Father was now the All-loving and the All-wise too. And as such, was ever after acknowledged by all living creatures,—gods and men, dwarfs and giants.

V.

THE STOLEN WINE.

Part I.

There had lain for ages upon ages, hidden away in the great rocky cellar of one of the giant's castles, a cask of wine, which had been stolen from the gods.

Never before had the gods been able to learn what had become of it; what giant had stolen it, nor in what castle it was hidden.

But now that Odin had become All-wise, nothing could be concealed from him.

"I know at last where the wine lies

hidden," said Odin one day to his son, Thor;
" and I shall set forth to find it."

Thor brought down his hammer with a
thud. " Let me go with you," cried he, springing up. " And let me fell to the earth with
one blow of my magic hammer the giant who
has stolen, and has kept hidden all these ages
our precious wine."

" No ; " answered Odin, " this time I must
go alone. The wine is guarded day and night,
and it will not be easy to bring it away, even
when I have found it. But watch for me,
dear son. One day there will come, beating
its wings against the shining gates of our city,
a great white eagle. Do not harm the eagle.
Open the gates to him ; for that eagle will be
Odin, returning with the stolen wine to our
city of Asgard."

Then Odin put aside his sparkling crown

and laid down his sceptre. His wonderful blue mantle, studded with stars and fastened always with a pale crescent moon, he also threw aside, and stepped forth in the garb of a common laborer. " It is in this guise that I shall win my way to the giant's castle," said Odin; and in a second he had passed out from the hall and was gone.

It was the giant, Suttung, that had stolen the wine, and it was in his castle that it had lain hidden all these years.

Now, of all the strong castles of all the giants, Suttung's castle was the strongest. The cellar was cut into the solid rock. Moreover, three sides of the castle rose in solid walls of granite; while the fourth, no less firm and strong, was built of massive blocks bound with hoops and bars and bolts of strongest iron and steel.

Now, Suttung had a brother, Bauge, who was a giant farmer. He kept nine strong slaves, half giants themselves, to do his work for him.

As Odin approached the fields of Bauge's farm, he saw the nine men hard at work.

"Your scythes are dull," said he, as he drew near.

"Yes, but we have no whetstone to sharpen them upon," answered the workmen, the great drops standing out upon their foreheads.

"I will sharpen them on mine," said Odin, drawing one from his pocket.

"It is a magic whetstone!" cried the men as they saw it work. "Give it to us. We need it more than you. Give it to us. Give it to us."

"Take it, then," answered Odin, throwing it high in the air and walking off.

"It is mine! It is mine! Let me have it! Give it to me! I will have it! Out of the way! It shall be mine!" screamed and quarreled the nine men as they pushed and crowded, each one determined to catch the whetstone as it came down to earth.

At last it fell. Then a fiercer battle followed. The angry men fell upon each other. They dragged and pulled and threw each other to the ground. They pounded each other; they struck at each other with their scythes. On and on they fought. Hour after hour the battle waged; till at last the Sun-god, in sheer dismay at so unloving a sight, hid his face behind the hills, and the nine men lay dead upon the fields.

It was an hour later when Odin reached the castle of Bauge.

"Can you give me shelter for the night?"

he asked, as the giant appeared at the door of his castle.

"Yes, I can give you shelter; but you must look elsewhere for your breakfast. A strange thing has happened. My nine slaves, while at work in the field, have fallen in battle upon each other, and have killed each other. Not one of them is left alive to serve me."

"They must have been idle, quarrelsome fellows," answered Odin.

"They were, indeed," answered Bauge; "but how shall I get my work done without them?"

"I will do the work for you," answered Odin.

"You! There is but one of you, even if you were willing to try," answered Bauge with but little interest.

"But I can do the work of any nine workmen that ever served you."

The giant laughed. "A remarkable workman. Pray, do you ask the wages of nine men as well?"

"I ask no wages," answered Odin. "I only ask that, as my pay when the work is done, you shall give me a draught of wine from the cask hidden in your brother's cellar."

Bauge stared. "How did you know there is a cask in my brother's cellar?" he gasped.

"It is enough that I know it," answered Odin coldly.

Bauge looked at Odin. "He is better than no man," he thought to himself. "I may as well get what work from him I can, before he finds that no being on earth can enter that cellar or force my brother to give away one drop of that wine."

"Very well, you may go to work," he said aloud. "I cannot promise you that we can make our way into my brother's cellar; but I will do what I can to help you."

"That is all I ask," answered Odin. "Now let me sleep, for I am tired; and if I am to do nine men's work, I must have nine men's sleep."

"And must you have nine men's food?" cried Bauge.

"I think it very likely," answered Odin with a queer smile. "Now let me sleep."

VI.

THE STOLEN WINE.

Part II.

"What is your name?" asked Bauge of his new workman when they set forth the next morning to the fields.

"You may call me Bolverk," answered Odin.

"Will one name be enough for all nine of you?" said Bauge with a disagreeable curling of his upper lip.

"I will not burden your giant mind with

more than one," Odin answered, — a funny little twinkle in his eye.

The giant gave a furious grunt. He did not quite know whether his new workman was stupid, or, whether under all his seeming meekness, it might not be that he was making fun of him.

Well, Bauge set Bolverk to work, and then, lazy fellow that he was, stretched himself out on a mountain side to watch.

"That new workman of mine," he bellowed, calling the attention of a neighbor giant to Odin at work in the field; "do you see him down there. among the corn? He says he can do nine men's work."

" A workman usually thinks himself equal to any nine other workingmen," roared back the neighbor. "Of course you have agreed to give him nine men's wages?"

Then the two giants roared with laughter.
They thought they had said a very bright
thing, and very likely they had. It is only
because you and I are mere earth-children that
we do not think so too.

As the days went on, Bauge began to
laugh less and to wonder more at his strange
workman. He worked on quietly from sunrise till sunset. He did not seem to hurry in
his work; he did not work over hours. But,
strange to say, the work went on, as the
workman had promised. No nine men could
have done more or could have done it better.

It was harvest time when Odin came;
the time when Frey, the god of the fields
and of all that grows, glides around among his
children and covers them over, or gathers in
their wealth and beauty. Like the kind,
loving father he is, he whispers to them now

of Njord who so soon will come, sweeping across the earth, breathing his cold freezing breath upon all the world, and covering it over with the cold white sheet that kills the flowers and the fruits. He teaches his children to curl themselves up beneath the earth until the cruel Njord is gone. For Njord seeks to kill the tiny leaves and buds, and shrivel the radiant flowers, that, through all the long warm summer days, have lifted their faces so brightly to their good friend, the Sun-god.

Perhaps it was because Frey and Odin worked together that there were such rare crops, and that the harvesting went on so smoothly. Certain it was that all the fields were cleared, the cellars were filled, and all was ready for the long, cold months to come, when cruel Njord was king.

Even Bauge was in good humor. " You

are indeed a wonderful workman," he said to Odin, as the last cellar was fastened and he sat down to rest.

"You are kind," answered Odin, the funny little twinkle coming again into his eyes. " Perhaps you would be willing to come with me now to your brother, that I may drink from the cask of wine that he keeps so closely guarded in his cellar."

Bauge began to feel uncomfortable. " He will not allow either you or me to so much as look upon that wine. You cannot have it."

" Bauge," said Odin, growing very tall and godlike, his wonderful eyes flashing with a light like fire, "you promised to do all you could to help me. Come and do as I bid you."

Bauge stared. His first thought was to kill the workman on the spot : but there was a something about him, he hardly knew what, that made him, instead, rise and follow Odin to the brother's castle.

" Tell me which cellar holds the wine," said Odin when they had reached the brother's mountain.

" This one," answered Bauge.

" Now take this augur. Make a hole with it through the solid wall."

Bauge obeyed like one in a dream. It was a magic augur. How it worked! How the powdered stone flew in a cloud about his face!

" This is a very —" Bauge stopped. What had become of his workman? Not a soul was in sight. Odin had disappeared. And to this day the giant never knew what became of him, nor does his brother know who stole his wine from the cellar.

The stupid Bauge stood staring, now at the augur, now at the hole in the wall. He saw a little worm climb up the wall and disappear through the hole. That is all he ever saw or ever knew.

The little worm laughed to itself as it crept in out of sight. "You are very stupid, Bauge, not to know me."

Reaching the inner side of the wall, the little worm stopped to look about. There stood the cask; and beside it sat the daughter of the giant. "Poor girl," said Odin—I mean, said the worm — to himself. "It is a bitter fate to be doomed to sit forever in this wretched dungeon watching your father's stolen treasure. But be happy. Soon you will be free. There will be no wine to watch."

The young giantess must have heard his words. For she looked up. There, just in front of the hole, the ray of light falling full upon his golden hair, stood a most beautiful youth. He looked so kindly upon her, and his eyes were so full of pity!

Her heart went out to him at once.

" I am very tired," said he gently. " So very tired. I have come a long, long distance. My home is far from here. I cannot tell you how far — but very, very far. If you would give me just one draught from the cask of wine."

The poor girl, grateful for the sound of a friendly voice, and for the sight of a human face, arose and lifted the lid for him.

Odin leaned over the cask. He put his lips to the wine and drank.

" You are very thirsty," said the giantess.

" Very," answered Odin, drinking on and on.

"You are very thirsty," said the giantess again.

"Very," answered Odin, still drinking on and on and on.

"You are very thirsty," said the giantess again; this time louder, her voice filled with fear.

"Very," answered Odin, still drinking on and on and on and on. Nor did he stop till every drop was gone and the cask stood dry and empty.

The young giantess, realizing all too late that the wine was stolen, ran to the cellar gateway, shouting as only a giant can shout for help.

The gateway flew open. In rushed the giants, Bauge and his brother.

"The wine! the wine!" they cried.

"Stolen, stolen!" sobbed the giantess, her sobs shaking even the solid cellar walls.

"The thief! The thief!" cried the giants. "Where is the thief?"

But there was no thief to be found. There stood the empty cask. But the thief? There was no living creature to be seen.

No living creature? I should not have said quite that. For there arose from a darkened corner of the cellar a beautiful, great white bird. Its wings brushed against the sides of the gateway as it passed. Then higher and higher, up, up, far, far away beyond the sea, above the clouds it soared, nor rested till its great wings beat against the golden bars of the shining gates of Asgard.

VII.

LOKE'S THEFT.

Thor was the son of Odin. He was a brave young god; and when the frost giants came sweeping down upon the shining city, none were more brave to fight for the protection of Asgard, the beautiful home of the gods, than Thor, the son of Odin.

There was another son, Loke A cruel, wicked, idle, evil-hearted god was he, the sorrow of his father Odin, the grief of his mother Frigg, and the terror of all the gods and goddesses.

Over this son the great Odin wept often bitter tears. More bitter still since he had drunk from the Well of Wisdom; for since then knowing, as he did, all things past and future, he knew that a day was yet to come, when, because of this wicked Loke, the light would go out from the earth; damp and cold and darkness would fall upon the shining city; the frost giants would overcome the gods; and there would come an end to all life. Nor was there any escape nor hope for any help. This fate, the Norns had decreed should be; and through the evil-hearted Loke it was to come.

In the golden hall of the gods dwelt Thor; and with him, his beautiful wife, Sif. Of all the goddesses there was none like her.

Her eyes were of heaven's own blue; and the light in them was borrowed from the stars. Her hair was of yellow, yellow gold; and as it lay massed above her pure white brow, it vied with the golden light of harvest time in softness and rich, deep color.

One happy peaceful day, when there was no danger abroad, and rest and peace had spread themselves above the halls of the city of Asgard, Sif lay sleeping. The Sungod's covering of soft warm rays fell upon her, and the leaves of Ygdrasil had spread themselves above her in tender, loving protection.

Loke, the idle one, angry and revengeful, as he always was, when happiness and rest and peace had driven out sorrow and care, paced angrily up and down the golden streets, his deep black frowns darkening even the clear, white light of heaven.

He came upon the beautiful sleeping wife of Thor.

"I hate my brother," he hissed through his cruel teeth. "And how proud he is of this golden hair of Sif's."

The wicked light flashed from his deep black eyes. Softly, like a thief, he crept towards the sleeping Sif. He seized the golden hair in his hand. A cruel smile shone over his evil face. "Boast now of your beauty, O Sif," he sneered. "Boast now of your Sif's golden hair, O Thor," he growled. And with one great sweep of his shining knife, he cut from the beautiful head the whole mass of gold.

It was late when Sif awoke. The leaves of Ygdrasil were moaning for the cruel deed. The Sun was sinking sorrowfully below the distant mountain peaks.

"O my gold! my gold!" sobbed Sif. "O who has stolen from me in my sleep my gold? O Thor, Thor! You were so proud of the gold. It was for you I prized it,— my beautiful, beautiful gold!"

At that second the voice of Thor was heard. His heavy call echoed across the skies and pealed from cloud to cloud. He was angry; for he had heard Sif's bitter cry and felt some harm had come to her.

"It is Loke that has done this," he thun-dered; and again his voice rolled from cloud to cloud. The very mountain peaks across the sea in the country of the Frost giants rocked and reeled. The waters foamed and tossed; the scorching lightnings flashed from his eyes; the whole sky was as one great sheet of fire.

The earth-children trembled as they had

never trembled before. Even Loke, shivering with fear, cowered behind the golden pillars of the great arched gateway.

"Forgive me, forgive me!" wailed he, as Thor flashed his great white light upon him.

"Out from your hiding place, O coward! Out! Out, or my thunderbolts shall strike you dead."

"Spare me, spare me!" groaned Loke. "Only spare me, and I will go down into the earth where the dwarfs do dwell —"

"Go!" thundered Thor, not waiting for the wretched god to finish. "Go, and bring back to me a crown of golden threads, woven and spun in the smithies of the dwarfs, that shall be as beautiful, and ten thousand times more beautiful, than the golden crown you have stolen from the head of Sif. Go to

them, tell them what you have done, and
never again enter the shining gateway of the
city of our Father Odin until you bring the
crown."

Loke slunk away, the thunders of the
wrath of Thor slowly, slowly following him.
The lightnings flashed dully across the skies.
The low rumbling of thunder, distant but
threatening, warned Loke that the wrath of
Thor was not appeased, neither would it be,
nor would there be any return to Asgard for
the evil doer, until the crown of gold was won.

DWARFS FORGING CROWN FOR LOKE.

VIII.

THOR'S HAMMER.

It was away down in the underground caves, and beneath the roaring waters of the rivers, and deep in the hearts of the mountains that these dwarf workmen dwelt, and worked their smithies, and spun their gold and brass.

"Make me a crown of gold for Sif the wife of Thor," snarled Loke, bursting in upon the workshop of the dwarfs.

The dwarfs were ugly little creatures, with crooked legs, and crooked backs. Their eyes were black, wicked little beads of eyes, and their hearts were malicious and some-times cruel. But they were the willing and ready slaves of the gods; and so, at even this ill-natured command from Loke, they set themselves to work.

The coals burned and blazed; the forges puffed and blew; the little workmen moulded and turned and spun their gold. Hardly had the Sun-god lifted his head above the castles of the frost giants, hardly had his light fallen upon the rich colors of the rainbow bridge, when Loke came forth from the underground caves, the shining crown in his hand.

Quickly he rose high in the air and stood before the gates of the city.

"Have you brought the crown?" thundered Thor from within the gates.

"I have brought the crown," answered

Loke in triumph. "And more than that," added he, when the gates had been opened to him, "I have brought as gifts from the dwarfs, a ship that will sail on land or sea and a spear that never fails. O there are no such workmen among any dwarfs as these who made the spear, the ship and the crown."

"You boast of what you do not know," croaked Brok, a little dwarf who stood near by.

"Who says I do not know?" cried Loke, turning sharply.

"I say you do not know," croaked the little dwarf again, his beadlike eyes snapping angrily, his whole crooked frame quivering with rage. "I have a brother, a workman in brass and gold, who can make gifts more pleasing to the gods than any you have brought."

Loke looked down upon the little dwarf in scorn. " Go to your brother," he sneered, "and bring to us the wonderful things you think he can make. Bring us one gift more wonderful than these I have, or more acceptable to Odin and Thor, and I will give your brother my head to pay him for his efforts." Then Loke roared with laughter, believing that he had made a rare, rich joke.

Hardly had the roars of laughter died away, when Brok, gliding down the rainbow bridge with a swiftness equalled only by the lightning, sprang into Midgard, and was making his way towards the great mountain beneath which worked the forges of his brother, the master-workman — Sindre.

"Some one cometh," said the dwarfs, pausing in their work to listen, their busy hammers in mid-air.

" Fear not," answered Brok, his harsh voice echoing down the great halls. " It is I — Brok — and I come to demand of you that now, if never again, you do your best; for Loke boasts to the gods of Asgard that no dwarfs in all the caverns of the under-world can make one gift more wonderful or more acceptable to Odin than those he brings — a crown of gold, a ship that will sail on land or sea, and a spear that never fails!"

A terrible roar burst forth from the hosts of angry dwarfs. "We will see! We will see!" they thundered. And seizing their hammers they set to work. The great forges blazed. The sparks flew. The smoke poured forth from the mountain top. Loke, looking out from the shining city, trembled. Well did he know the workmanship of these dwarfs of Brok; and well did he know how rash had been his scornful promise to the angry little dwarf.

"We will make a hammer for Thor," said Sindre, the greatest among the workmen in this under world; "a hammer, that when thrown from his mighty hand, shall ring through all the heavens. A trail of fire shall follow it. Its aim shall never fail; and it shall carry death and destruction wherever it falls.

"Blow thou the bellows, Brok; and I myself will mould the hammer from the red hot iron."

With Brok at the bellows, the very mountain rocked, and Midgard for miles about was ablaze with the blaze of light from the mountain top.

"This shall not be," snarled Loke. And rushing down from Asgard he crouched outside the great, black cave to listen.

"A hammer for Thor!" Those were the words he heard. The ugly face grew uglier. An instant, and there was no Loke at the cavern mouth; but instead, a poisonous, stinging gadfly, whose green back glistened, and whose shining wings buzzed and hummed with cruelty and revenge. There was a hard, ringing tone of defiance in their singing, and the tone was like that of the voice of Loke himself.

"You shall drop the bellows," buzzed the gadfly bitterly, as it alighted upon the neck of Brok.

It was a cruel sting; and its poison forced, even from the sturdy Brok, a cry of pain.

"I know you. It is Loke," he cried; "but I will not drop the bellows though you sting me through and through and with a thousand stings!"

The gadfly buzzed with rage. Straight towards the hand upon the bellows it darted. Brok groaned again. His face grew pale; he quivered with the pain; still he held the mighty bellows and worked the roaring forge.

"You will not!" hissed the gadfly; and again it drove its poison sting, this time straight between the eyes of the suffering dwarf. And now Brok staggered. His hands relaxed their hold. Blinded with pain, he dropped the bellows. The blood ran down his face. The gadfly still hummed and buzzed.

"You have nearly spoiled it," cried Sindre. "Why did you drop the bellows? See how short the handle is! And how rough! But it cannot be helped now; nor will its terror be any less to Loke. Ha, ha, I would have made it handsome; but there is a power in it that shall make even the gods tremble in all the ages to come. Hurry away with it, and place it in Thor's mighty hands. And here are other gifts. Take them all, and bring me Loke's head. He has promised. Surely even he must keep his word, wicked and deceitful though he is."

Brok seized the hammer, and, with the gifts, hurried up through the dark cavern, out into the light of Midgard, up the rainbow bridge, and, with triumph in his swarthy face, sprang into the presence of the great god Odin.

Loke roared with laughter at the sight of the awkward, clumsy hammer; but there was a proud, confident look in the dwarf's shining eyes that Loke did not like; and, coward that he was, his heart began already to fail him.

"Let us see the gifts," said Odin, "that

we may judge which workman among the dwarfs has proved himself most wonderful."

"First of all," said Loke, coming forward, "Here is the golden crown for Sif."

Eagerly Thor seized the crown, and placed it upon poor Sif's head.

"Wonderful! wonderful!" cried all the gods, for straightway the golden hair began to grow to Sif's head, and in a second it was as if her golden locks had never been stolen from her.

"To you, O Odin," said the dwarf, now coming forward, "I give this ring of gold. It is a magic ring; and each night it will cast off from itself another ring, as pure and as heavy, as round and as large as itself."

"What is that," sneered Loke, "compared with this? See, O Father Odin, I bring you a magic spear. Accept this, my second gift. It is a magic spear that never fails."

" But behold my second gift," interrupted Brok. " It is a boar of wonderful strength. It, too, is magic. No horse can run, no bird can fly with such speed. It travels both on land and sea; and in the night its bristles shine with such a light, that it matters not how dense the blackness, the forest or the plain will be as bright as noonday."

" I, too, have a gift that will travel on land or sea," cried Loke, pushing himself forward again. " See, it is a ship. And not only will it travel on land or sea, but it can lift itself and sail like a bird above the clouds and through the air."

" It will be hard indeed to say which gift is greatest," said Odin kindly.

" Look now, O, Odin, and Frigg and Thor and Sif and all the gods, at this the last of my three gifts. This hammer, O Thor, I

bring to you, the god of thunder. Strike with
it, and your thunders shall echo and re-echo
from cloud to cloud as never they were heard
before. Thrown into the air or at a foe, like
Loke's spear, it shall never miss its aim; but,
more than that, it shall return always to the
hand of Thor. No foe can conceal it, no foe
can destroy it. It will never fail thee, O Thor,
thou god of thunder."

"But what a clumsy handle," sneered
Loke, who already began to fear the hammer
was to win the favor of the gods.

"Yes," answered Brok, "the handle is
clumsy and it is short. But none knows
better than you why it is so."

Loke colored and moved uneasily. "Do
not think," continued Brok, "that I do not
know it was you who sent the poisonous
gadfly to sting and bite me as I worked at the

blazing forge, pounding out the brass and gold from which this hammer is made.

"You thought to pain me into giving up this contest, you coward! you evil one! you boaster!

"When the handle was welded just so far, you drove the gadfly into my eye. I could not see to finish the work; but although the handle is short and clumsy, the magic power is there, and with it in his hand, no power in earth or among the frost giants even can overcome our great god Thor."

A ringing shout of joy arose from the gods. Thor swung his hammer over his head and threw it far out against the clouds. The thunder rolled, the clouds filled with blackness, and the lightnings flashed, as the magic hammer, humming through the air, came back to the hands of Thor.

"Now give me my wager," cried Brok.
"I was promised the head of Loke."

"Take it," laughed Loke. "Take it."

Brok drew near. "I will take it," is
hissed through his set teeth; "and a rich day
will it be both in Midgard and in Asgard
when your miserable head is bound down in
the home of the dwarfs of the underground
world."

"But halt," commanded Loke. "My head
you may have; but you must not touch my
neck. One drop of blood from that, and you
forfeit your life."

Brok stood for a moment white with
anger. He knew that he was foiled. Then
springing forward, he thundered, "I may not
touch your neck; but see, I have my
revenge." And so, falling upon Loke, who
struggled, but struggled in vain, he whipped

from his mantle a thong and thread of brass; and before even Loke knew what had been done, he had sewed, firm together, the lying boasting lips of the evil god, Loke, the wicked-hearted son of Odin.

THOR.

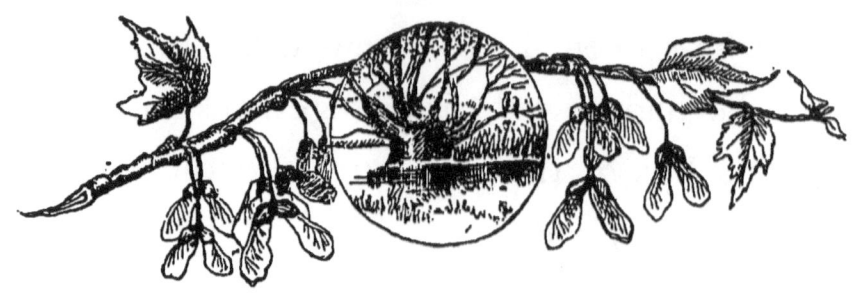

THE THEFT OF THE HAMMER.

XI.

It was to the sweet and loving god Baldur that the earth owed its warmth and beauty, its rich fruit and its rare harvests. How the frost giants hated Baldur, and how they struggled year after year to wrest the earth from him!

They hated the warmth Baldur brought with him, for it destroyed their power. They hated the sweet flowers and the soft grass and the tiny leaves that everywhere peeped out when the winds whispered, " Baldur is coming, Baldur is coming."

But no sooner had Baldur turned away and said, " Good-bye, dear Earth, for a little time, remember Baldur loves you and will come back again to you," than the frost giants would creep out from their mountain gorges, and burst forth upon the fields and forests.

The tiny bubbling brooks they would seal with their cruel chains of ice; even the great rivers could not hold their freedom against the giant power.

Like angry fiends they would seize upon the leaves and tear them from the trees. The tiny flowers hung their heads and shriveled with fear when they approached; nor were the frost giants content until the whole earth lay brown and cold and barren beneath their hand. Then, all beauty swept away, they covered over all, their silent sheet of snow, and stood, grim sentinels, cold and hard, guarding their work of destruction and desolation.

There was deep silence when the frost giants reigned; no sound was heard save the sad moaning among the branches of the forest, as the firs and pine trees bent towards each other and whispered of the days when Baldur shone upon them.

But the frost giants never yet had conquered; never yet had Baldur failed to return to the trees and flowers and rivers and streams that he loved so well.

At his first step upon the ice, a crackling sound was heard — a sound which awoke the sleeping earth and warned the frost giants to flee to their mountains.

"Baldur has come! Baldur has come!"

the birds and every living thing would cry; and a rustle and sound of music would thrill the waiting earth.

Then came always a mighty battle. The frost giants lashed the waters and rocked the trees. The winds shrieked, the sky grew cold and black. The snows fell and the driving rain beat against the earth. But Baldur, the quiet, firm, loving Baldur always conquered. How, he himself could hardly tell. He did not fight; he did not storm. He only bent his shining face over the struggling earth and waited.

Little by little, when their fury was spent, the frost giants, defiant but conquered, retreated. The great sheets of ice broke up, and the rivers rushed forth singing their mad songs of joy and freedom. The snows faded away, and one by one the little flowers peeped forth again.

All now was happiness and warmth and fragrance; the flowers bloomed; the fruits turned mellow; the sky grew warm; and the pines and fir trees breathed deep sighs of rest and contentment that once again sweet Baldur was among them.

And not only did the frost giants hate Baldur, but they hated Frey, who often robbed them of the fruits and flowers they loved to breathe their bitter breath upon and kill. Thor, too, they hated; for with his magic hammer, he now, more than ever, loved to bring forth the lightnings and the thunder, and to send down upon the earth refreshing showers of soft, warm rain.

As the frost giants scowled down from their icy castles, and saw the little flowers turn up their happy faces to drink in the sparkling drops, and heard the birds trill their happy songs, and smelled the rich fragrance of the damp firs and pines, they roared with anger and vexation.

"Let us revenge ourselves upon this insolent Thor who robs us of our rights," they bellowed to each other across the great valleys that separated their giant peaks.

"We can do nothing so long as he holds the magic hammer," growled one.

"We must steal the hammer from him," shouted another.

"Steal the hammer! Steal the hammer!" shouted all the giants until the very skies echoed with the words.

"And I will be the one to steal it," bellowed Thrym, the strongest and greatest giant of them all.

"And, moreover, I will go at once to the city of Asgard. The gods are asleep. With

my great eye, I can see even now the hammer
lying beside the sleeping Thor.   Guard **my**
castle.   I am gone."

THE THEFT OF THE HAMMER.

And putting on the guise of a great bird,
Thrym spread his wings and flew across the
black night to Asgard. The gods shivered in
their sleep as he entered and breathed his
breath upon the summer air of heaven, but
knew not what had chilled them.

In the morning there was a heavy frost upon the gateways. There was a chill in the air. For Thrym, the frost giant, had crept in upon them. He had crept even to the hall in which the mighty Thor was sleeping. He had crept close beside the mighty god — and the magic hammer was gone.

THOR AND LOKE ON THE JOURNEY AFTER THE HAMMER.

XII.

THE FINDING OF THE HAMMER.

"My hammer! My hammer!" thun dered Thor, awaking and finding it gone.

The gods in all Asgard awoke with a start.

"What a crash of thunder! So quick,

so sharp!" cried the earth-people; for they did not know it was a cry of rage from Thor.

"Loke," thundered Thor again. "Put you on wings. Go you to the home of the Frost giants and bring back my hammer. Some one of them has stolen it. Go! Go! I say."

And Loke, who had been a very obedient servant to Thor since his theft of the golden hair of Sif, put on the magic wings and fled away.

"What brings you here in the land of the Frost giants?" growled Thrym, as Loke alighted before him.

"I have come for the hammer you have stolen from Thor," answered Loke boldly, seeing at once, from the jeering look in Thrym's eye, that he was the thief.

"You will never find it," sneered Thrym.

FREYJA IN HER CHARIOT.

" It is well hidden ; but I will send it back to you if Odin will send me Freyja for my wife."

Loke begged and coaxed and threatened ; but it was all of no avail. " Never," bellowed Thrym, " until you send Freyja to me."

" She shall go," thundered Thor, when Loke came back to Asgard. " Whatever the price, the hammer must be brought back. Asgard is not safe without it."

But Freyja was as fierce as had been Thrym himself. " I will not go," she insisted. " Never! Never! Never will I go!"

" I say you must," thundered Thor. But although Thor's thunders were terrible and his frown was deep and inky black, Freyja was not to be moved either by pleading or threatening.

" Go yourself," said she. " Dress yourself as a goddess and go." Nor would she listen even to another word. Thor thundered and rumbled and rolled. It was all of no avail. Freyja was a goddess and would not be driven.

"I will go," said Thor at last. "Bring me a bridal dress. Hang a necklace around my neck. Bind a bridal veil about my head. The giants are as stupid as they are large; and I will set forth in the name of Freyja to meet the giant Thrym."

Thor was quickly dressed, and the bridal party set forth across the sky in the chariot of the Sungod. How the thunder rolled! How the lightnings flashed from the angry eyes of Thor! How he grumbled and rumbled!

Jotunheim was reached. The Sungod lowered his chariot behind the hills; and a soft, red light spread over the earth and sky as the bridal party entered the castle of the giant Thrym.

"Freyja has come! Freyja has come!"
bellowed Thrym. "Come, come, everyone to
the bridal feast! Come, come to the feast of
Thrym and Freyja!"

The giants in all the mountains round
about answered to the call of Thrym. An
hour, and the huge castle was filled with the
huge guests. A great feast was held. But
through it all Thor sat silent and motionless.
Indeed, he dared not move; he dared not
speak lest the thunder burst forth from his
lips, or the lightning shoot forth from his eyes.

"Now lift the veil from Freyja's face,"
bellowed Thrym, when all save the bride her-
self had eaten and drank their fill. "Let me
see the eyes of my bride. Let us all look
upon the face of my goddess bride."

"Not yet," whispered Loke coming forward; "it was the command of Thor that the

veil should not be lifted, nor should you claim Freyja for your own, until the hammer was placed in her hand, to be returned to the gods."

· "Bring in the hammer! Bring in the hammer!" roared Thrym, full of loud, good humor.

The hammer was brought. Hardly could Thor wait to have it placed in his hand.

His thunder began to rumble. There was a dangerous light in his eyes; but Thrym and the guests saw none of this. But hardly was the hammer within his reach when forth Thor sprang, seized it in his clutched fingers, tore aside the bridal veil, and with a rumble and a roar that shook the mountains of Jotun-heim and razed the great stone castles to the ground, he poured out his lightnings upon the giants, one and all. Right and left he swung the mighty weapon; the giants quaked and trembled with terror; Thrym ran and hid

himself behind a mountain; the air was white
with lightning; the hills rang with the crash-
ings of the thunder; the seas lashed and
foamed and answered back the echoes; the
walls of Jotunheim shook and trembled.

And now the chariot of the Sungod was
near at hand. Into it Thor and Loke leaped,
and were borne back to the city of the gods.
The hammer was restored. Again Thor held
it in his mighty grasp. He held it, and
Asgard once more was safe.

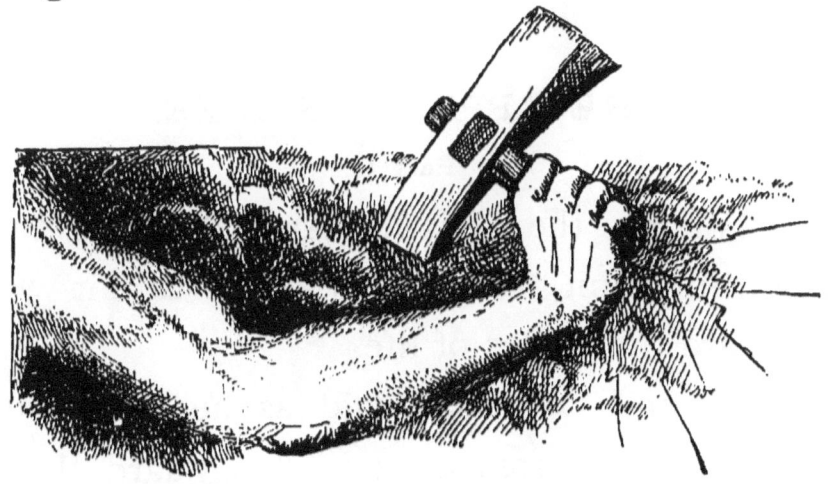

XIII.

THE APPLES OF LIFE.

Part I.

Among the gods in Asgard, dwelt the beautiful Idun, the goddess whose care it was to guard the apples of life.

"Idun," Odin, had said as he gave into her hands the rosy apples, "to guard these apples and keep them forever from all harm, is to do a greater service for Asgard than even Thor, with his mighty thunders, or Baldur, with his warm light, can do; for these are the apples of everlasting youth. Without them, what would Asgard be more than the cities of Midgard or of Jotunheim? What would the gods be more than the mortals of Midgard or the giants of Jotunheim? So guard them well, beautiful Idun, for to them you owe your beauty, even as we owe to them our never fading youth."

One day, when all was quiet and peaceful and happy in the city of Asgard, Loke, feeling within him the stirring of his own evil heart, betook himself to Midgard in search of mischief. The peace and quiet of Asgard he could no longer endure. Then, too, it was to him a cruel delight to shoot his arrows into

the lives of the helpless children of Midgard
and make them sad.

O, Loke was a cruel god! "Surely," Odin
would sometimes say, as he looked upon him
and thought of the wretchedness that yet
would fall on Asgard through Loke's wicked
deeds, "surely, Loke has the spirit of a Frost
giant; and the Frost giants are bitter, bitter
foes to Asgard."

This day Loke longed. for mischief. "I
will go down to Midgard and find some happy
heart to sadden," said he, his eyes shining
with their wicked light.

Down the rainbow bridge he hastened,
and, with a light bound, sprang upon a bright
tree in the beautiful land of Midgard.

"Who are you?" cried he, seeing in the
tree beside him a great, white bird.

But the bird made no reply; he only

winked, and blinked, and stared at Loke, and
crooned, and pruned his feathers.

"Do you not know a god speaks to you?"
stormed Loke, growing angry even with a bird.

Still no answer.

"Was ever there such a stupid bird?
Indeed, like the people of Midgard, you seem
to have no wisdom," sneered Loke. And
determined to vent his evil mood, he seized a
branch and began to beat the bird.

Then a strange thing happened. The
bird, who all this time had seemed so stupid —
too stupid even to fly away — now seized
upon the bough and held it fast. Loke pulled
and pulled with all his godlike strength. He
could not move it; it was as if held in the
grasp of a giant.

"Stupid bird!" sneered Loke, when he
found he could do the bird no harm. "I will

not stay in the tree with such a stupid creature."

A strange sound — almost like a laugh of triumph — squeezed itself out from the beak of the big bird.

"Go, Loke, go at once. Go back to Asgard; or perhaps you would like to go with me to Jotunheim," spoke the bird at last. And as he spoke, he spread his wings, and arose high in the air. Alas, alas for Loke, as the bird rose, he rose too; nor could he free himself. He screamed, he fought, he begged, he strove with all his godlike arts to free himself, but all in vain.

On, on they flew, the bird and Loke, across the sky, over and under and between the clouds, across the great wide sea, at last across the snow-white peaks, down, down to a castle in Jotunheim, in the land of the mighty

Frost giants, the terrible, the dreaded enemies of the gods.

"Let me free! Let me free!" foamed Loke, struggling against the bird, whose magic held him fast.

"I will never let you free," answered the bird, throwing off his disguise and standing forth a giant foe; "I will never let you free except on one condition."

"I grant it! I grant it! Whatever it is, I grant it," cried the coward, caring for nothing but to free himself.

"The condition is this," continued the giant coolly: "I will let you free if you will bring me, without delay, the apples of ever-lasting youth—the apples that Idun guards and watches over, locked so closely in the golden casket in the city of Asgard.

Loke stared. He caught his breath. To

give up the apples of life — the fruit by which the gods were kept forever young and strong and beautiful, — that was too great a thing to ask even of Loke, evil as he was.

"There are no such apples," answered he, trying, as cowards always do, to hide himself behind a lie. "There are no such apples."

"Very well," answered the giant, opening a great dungeon door, and thrusting Loke in. "When you are ready to do what I say, you may come out; never until then." The great dungeon door creaked upon its terrible hinges and Loke was alone, a prisoner, at the mercy of the Frost giant.

Loke howled and beat against the walls of the dungeon.

"Are you ready to do what I asked of you?" asked the Frost giant, opening the great door the next morning.

"There are no such apples," cried Loke. "On my honor as a god, I swear it!"

The giant made no reply. The heavy door creaked again, and Loke was alone.

"Are you ready to do what I asked of you?" asked the Frost giant, opening the great door the second morning.

"Anything in all Asgard, O Giant, I promise you—anything but the apples," cried Loke.

The giant made no reply. The heavy door creaked again, and Loke was alone.

"Are you willing to do what I asked of you?" asked the Frost giant, opening the great door the third morning.

"One of the apples, O Giant, I might steal from Idun and escape with before the fruit was missed," Loke began.

The giant made no reply. The heavy door creaked again and Loke was alone.

"Are you ready to do what I asked of you?" asked the Frost giant, opening the great door the fourth morning.

"Yes, two of the three apples will I promise to bring you. With even one left, the gods might be content; for even then their lives would be far longer than the life of mortals."

The giant made no reply. The heavy door creaked again and Loke was alone.

"Are you ready to do what I asked of you?" asked the Frost giant, opening the great door the fifth morning.

"Yes," answered Loke, meekly.

"You are willing to bring the apples of life?"

"Yes."

"And you will bring all three of them?"

"Yes."

"And you will bring them at once?"

"Yes."

"Go, then. I will go with you. Outside the walls of the shining city I will wait for you to bring the apples to me."

Then putting on the guise of birds, the two set forth, reaching the gateway of the city just as the Sungod was pouring down his flood of red and golden light upon the shining spires. The whole city lay bathed in the sunset splendor.

" Idun," said Loke, going directly to her, " it is well you guard so closely these golden apples of life. Without them we should grow old and die, even as wretched mortals grow old and die."

" Indeed, it would fare ill with us if harm came to these precious apples," answered Idun. " See the rich bloom upon them. If that were lost, then would our bloom be lost as well, and we should grow old and wrinkled."

" Yes," answered Loke; " and still,— it seems very strange — but outside the gate of our city, just on the outer walls, are growing apples, looking so like these I cannot tell them one from the other. Bring your apples with you and let us see if they are alike. If they should prove to be, then I will gather them for you, and we will put them all together in the golden casket."

" How strange ! " thought Idun innocently.

" The Frost giant, in his great bird guise, wheeled round and round, impatiently awaiting the coming of Idun and the apples. Hardly had the gates closed upon her, when down he swooped, seized her in his great strong beak, and flew with her across the sea to his home among the mountains.

The days rolled on and on. The Sungod rose, and drove his chariot across the sky, and sank behind the distant purple hills a thousand times.

There was a gloom, a shadow over Asgard ; for the gods were growing old. The life had gone out of their eyes ; their smooth round faces had grown thin and peaked ; their step was halting, and the feebleness of age was falling upon them.

"It is Loke who has done this," thundered Thor one day, when, from old age and weakness, he had been defeated in a battle with the now ever youthful giants. "It is Loke who has done this, and we will bear it no longer. Look at Odin; even he grows weak and bent and trembling. He is like the old men in Midgard. He, Odin, the All-father."

Thor's indignation waxed stronger and stronger. He set forth in search of Loke. "I will not even wait for him to come," he thundered, seizing his hammer and setting forth. I shall find him, the evil-hearted, somewhere making mischief among the innocent people of Midgard," said he.

XIV.

THE APPLES OF LIFE.

Part II.

" Henceforth, O evil-hearted, cruel Loke," burst forth the angry Thor, " henceforth Thor guards the walls of Asgard. Midgard, the skies, he shall forsake; no more will he brew storms; never shall the thunder roll nor the lightnings flash; for Thor will watch forever upon the battlements of Asgard the approach of the evil god who has brought such grief upon us. Never shall he enter the gates of the city again. Let him dare approach even to the golden gates, and Thor will smite him with his mighty hammer."

Loke quailed before the fury of the great god Thor. To be an outcast from Asgard, even he could not bear. "Spare me, spare me!" whined the cowardly Loke. "Spare me once more, and I will go again to Jotunheim. I will bring back Idun and the three apples of life."

Thor stood looking at the cowardly Loke. He longed to strike him with the hammer; to kill him with his thunder bolt; to scorch him with his lightning arrows. But, evil as he was, Loke was immortal; he was the son of Odin.

"Go, then, you mischief-making, evil-hearted son of unhappy Odin! Go; and whether success is yours or not, remember Thor guards the walls of Asgard and watches with his thunders for your return. Never, never, as long as Thor wields the mighty hammer, and holds the powers of thunder and

lightning, shall Loke enter the golden city without the golden apples of immortal life."

Without another word, Loke put on his guise of a great white bird and sped across

the sea and sky, again to the land of Jotunheim.

Straight down he swooped upon the
castle of the giant who, all this time, had kept
Idun imprisoned in a strong walled tower of
solid rock.

The giant was out upon the sea. " And
it is well for me," thought Loke, "that he is.
No power in Midgard or in Asgard could
wrest these precious apples from the giant's
grasp."

One quick look out over the mountains
and down upon the sea, and Loke seized Idun
in his talons, changed her at once into a nut,
the apples safe within the shell, and swept
away towards Asgard.

But alas for Loke! The giant had heard
the whirr of the great white wings. Leaping
to his feet in his boat, he scanned the sky

with his sharp giant eye. "It is Loke! It is Loke!" bellowed he, catching sight of the great white bird among the clouds. "It is Loke! It is Loke! No bird of Midgard flies so high nor sweeps the air with such mighty wings."

With one great giant pull, he shot his boat upon the shore; with one great giant bound he struck the mountain top.

"The apples of life! the apples of life!" he thundered. "Gone! gone! The apples of life are gone!"

One second, and putting on the guise of a great grey eagle he shot up into the sky in swift pursuit of Loke. The Sungod hid his chariot behind a cloud that the shadows might protect and cover Loke. Thor sent forth his thunder. The skies blackened; the wind beat back the great grey eagle; the lightnings

staggered and blinded him.   Still on and on
he flew, gaining in spite of all upon the track
of Loke.

Every eye in Asgard was strained; every
giant in Jotunheim stood breathless upon his
mountain.   The great round faces of the
giants grew tense; the wrinkled aged faces of
the gods grew pale.   It was a terrible race.
It was a race for life and health and ever-
lasting youth.

"Build fires upon the walls!   Heap up
the brush!   Stand ready with the tapers!"
cried Odin, who foresaw the end.

The brush is heaped.   Each god stands
ready, his haggard face growing whiter and
thinner with fright and dread and eagerness.

Already the rush of Loke's wings are
heard.   The eagle follows close.   Nearer and
nearer they come, closer and closer is the race.

One moment more! — One second! — The frightened eyes of Loke can be seen, so near he is. Thor sends his blinding fire once more across the eagle's track. It reels, for an instant it falls back. In that one second, with one last mighty stroke, Loke clears the walls and falls, exhausted, breathless, almost dead upon the golden pavement of the city.

"The fires! the fires! the fires!" cried Odin. An instant, and there rises from the walls great sheets of blaze. The brush crackles and snaps and sends up great tongues of fire. The eagle, angry, desperate, and blinded by the lightning sweeps on, straight towards them. Like a foolish moth, he bears down upon the city, into the very heart of the blaze. A sudden crackling, a cry of pain, a cloud of black, black smoke, and the great grey eagle falls a helpless mass upon the pavement beside the breathless Loke.

The haggard faces flush with hope and joy. The apples are safe. Idun has come back, the apples again are theirs, and life and joy and eternal youth once more are with them.

Now the goddess of music bursts forth again in song; the god of poetry pours forth his melody; a feast is spread, and the gods and goddesses once more eat of the wonderful apples of life. The color comes back into their faded cheeks; light again flashes from their eyes. Youth and health and strength are theirs again. Peace reigns once more in Asgard.

LOKE'S WOLF.

Although the Apples of Life had been brought back, and although Loke appeared for some time very penitent and willing to obey the laws of the kind Odin, the gods had little faith in him. More than that, so much had they suffered, that now they were in constant fear of him. "We never know," plead Freyja and Sif and Idun, all of whom had good reason to fear him, "what mischief he may be planning."

And so it came about that Loke was driven forth from Asgard, as indeed he deserved to be.

Straight to the home of the giants Loke went — he always had been a giant at heart, the evil creature! — and was much more in harmony with them in their thoughts and acts, than ever he had been with the gods whom he claimed as his people.

But now that he was cast out from Asgard, and could no longer share its beauties and its joys, he had but one wish — that was, to be revenged upon the gods, to destroy them, and to ruin their golden city.

To do this he raised two dreadful creatures. Terrible monsters! Even the gods shuddered as they looked upon them.

"Loke! Loke!" thundered Odin, looking down upon him in wrath that he should dare such vengeance.

But Loke stood defiant. There was but one thing to be done, so the gods thought;

and that was to take these terrible creatures from Loke's power.

"The serpent we will cast into the sea," said Thor. "But the wolf — what shall we do with the wolf? Certainly he cannot be left to wander up and down in Midgard. The sea would not hold him. Loke must not have him in Jotunheim. What shall be done with him?"

"Kill him," said some.

"No," answered Odin. "To him Loke has given the gift of everlasting life. He will not die as long as we the gods have life. There is but one way left open to us; and that is to bring the wolf into Asgard. Here we can watch him and keep him from much, if not all the evil he would do."

And so the wolf — the Fenris-wolf he was called — was brought into the home of the gods.

He was a dreadful creature to look upon. His eyes were like balls of fire; and his fangs were white, and sharp, and cruel.

Every day he grew more terrible. Fiercer and fiercer he grew, and larger and stronger and more dreadful to look upon.

"What is to be done with him?" asked Odin one day, his face white with despair, as he looked upon the wolf, and realized what sorrow by and by he would bring among them.

" Kill him!" cried one.

" Send him to Jotunheim," cried another.

" Chain him," thundered Thor. And indeed to chain him seemed really the only thing that could be done with him.

"We will make the chains this night," said Thor. And at once the great forge was set in motion. All night long Thor worked the forge, hammering with his mighty hammer the links that should make a chain to hold the Fenris-wolf.

Morning came. The gods were filled with hope as they saw the great heap of iron. "Now we shall be safe. Now we shall be free," they said; for no creature living can break the irons that the god of Thunder forges."

The wolf growled and showed his wicked teeth as Thor approached and threw the chain about him. He knew the gods hated him and feared him. He knew, too, that, with his wondrous strength, even the chains of Thor were not too strong for him to break.

So, snarling and showing his fangs and lashing his tail, he allowed himself to be bound. "They are afraid of me," the cruel wolf grinned. "And well they may be;

there is a power in me that even they do not yet dream of."

The chains were tightly fastened, and the gods waited eagerly for the wolf to test his strength with them.

Now, the wolf knew well enough that there were no chains that could hold him. " I will amuse myself," said he to himself, " by tormenting the gods." So he glared at the chains with his fiery eyes, sniffed here and there at them, lifted one paw and then the other, bit at them with his sharp teeth, and clawed at them with his strong claws ; setting up now and then a howl that echoed, like the thunders of Thor, from cloud to cloud across the skies.

The faces of the gods grew brighter and brighter. They looked at each other and hope rose high in their hearts. "We are saved!"

they whispered to each other. "Hear how he howls! He knows he cannot break chains forged in the smithy of the mighty Thor."

But Odin did not smile. He knew only too well that the wolf was amusing himself; and that when the gods were least expecting it, he would spring forth and shatter the links of the mighty chain, even as a mortal might shatter a chain of straw.

"Conquered at last, you cruel Fenris-wolf!" thundered Thor, lifting his hammer in scorn, to throw at the helpless wolf.

"The Fenris-wolf is never conquered," hissed the wolf; and with one bound he leaped across the walls of Asgard, down, down across the skies to Midgard, the links of the chains scattering like sparks of fire as he flew through the air.

"See! See!" cried the people of Midgard, as they saw the fiery eyes of Fenris gleam across the sky. " See ! A star has fallen ! A star has fallen into the sea !" For the people of Midgard cannot understand the wonders of the heavens and the mysteries of the gods.

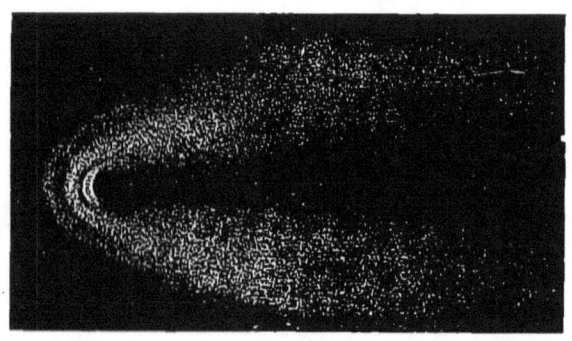

The gods stood, wonder-struck. Their faces were pale with fright. The brow of Thor grew black and stern. Odin looked pityingly upon them all. " Lose not your courage," said he kindly. " The Fenris-wolf shall yet be bound; and there shall yet remain to us ages upon ages of happiness and freedom from his wicked power. Go now to the dwarfs who work their forges in the great mines beneath the mountains of Midgard. They shall make for you a magic chain that even Fenris cannot break."

Hardly were the words out of Odin's mouth when Thor set forth upon the wings of his own lightning, to the home of the dwarfs, to do the bidding of Odin the All-wise.

XVI
THE FENRIS WOLF.
Part II.

With wonderful speed the chain was forged; and when the Sun-god lifted his head above the hills, to send forth his light again across the fields of Midgard, the first sight that greeted his return was Thor, a great mass of golden coil within his hand, speeding up the rainbow bridge to Asgard.

It was a tiny chain — hardly larger than a thread; but in it lay a magic strength.

Entering the great golden gate, Thor saw the Fenris wolf, again creeping stealthily up and down the streets.

Thor's hand shut tight upon the handle of his hammer. It was hard to believe that a blow from the hammer would not slay the wicked creature. For an instant Thor's face grew black. Then forcing a smile, and showing to the wolf the mass of gold, he said, "Come Fenris; come with me into the hall. There the gods are to meet and test our strength upon this magic coil. Whoever breaks it, and so proves himself the strongest, is to win a prize from the great All-father Odin."

The wolf stretched back his cruel lips, and showed his sharp fangs of teeth. He did not speak; but his wicked grin said, "You do not deceive the Fenris-wolf."

Together Thor and the Fenris-wolf entered the presence of Odin and the gods and goddesses.

"I have," said Thor, "a magic coil. It is very strong. The dwarfs made it for me; and Odin has promised a great prize to the one who shall be strong enough to break its links. Come, let us try."

Then the gods —for they all understood what Thor was about to do — sprang forward, seizing the coil, pulling and twisting it in every way and in every direction, coiling it about the pillars of the hall, and hanging by it from the arches; until at last, tired out and breathless, they sank exhausted upon the golden floors.

"Fenris," called Thor. "Now is your time to prove to us what you have so often said — that you are stronger than we. Try if you can break this golden thread which, small as it is, has proved too strong for the strength of the gods."

The wolf growled. He did not care to risk even his strength in a magic coil. He growled and slunk away.

"What! Fenris, are you a coward? After all your boasted strength, why is it that you shrink from a contest in which the gods have willingly taken part? Do you mean to say that, because the gods have been defeated, you fear that you, too, may be defeated?"

The wolf halted. He looked back at the gods and growled a long, low growl. The words of Thor had stung his pride.

Thor laughed. "O Fenris, Fenris! this is your boasted strength! your boasted courage! To slink away in a contest with the gods—the gods at whose strength you have always sneered and scoffed."

"Fenris is a coward!" cried all the gods; and the heavens echoed with their laughter.

This was more than the wolf could bear. Back he sprang into the hall.

"I hear your sneers," he snarled. "I hear you call me coward. Give me the cord; bind me with it round and round; fasten me to the strongest pillar of this great hall. If the coil is an honest coil, Fenris can break it. There is no chain he cannot break. But if you are blinding me — if you have here a cord woven with magic such as no power can break — how am I to know? I put this test to you. Some one of you shall place your hand between my jaws. As long as that hand is there, you may coil and coil the thread about me. Then, if I find the cord a magic cord, Fenris shall set his teeth upon the hand and crush it."

The gods stared at one another. Surely, Thor must not lose his hand. Thor needed his hand with which to wield the magic hammer.

Then Tyre, the brave god Tyre, the god
of courage and bravery and unselfishness
stepped forth.

"Here is my hand, O Fenris-wolf. It
shall be yours to destroy if you can not loose
yourself when bound in the golden coil."

Again the Fenris-wolf showed his shining
teeth. He seized the hand between his heavy
jaws; Thor bound the cord about him. "Now
free yourself," he thundered. "Free yourself,
and prove to the gods the mighty power of the
Fenris-wolf."

The wolf, his eyes blazing with wrath,
and with fear as well, struggled with the coil.
But alas for the wolf! And joy for the gods!
The harder he struggled, the fiercer he battled,
the tighter drew the cord. With a howl of
rage that shook the city and echoed even to
the base of the great Mt. Ida, he seized upon

the hand of Tyre and tore it from his wrist. With another angry howl he sprang towards Thor; but with a quick turn Thor seized one end of the coil, fastened it to a great rock, and before the wolf could set his fangs he hurled him, rock and all, over the walls of the city, down down into the mighty sea.

"And there, chained to his rocky island, he shall abide forever," cried the gods; "and now peace once more shall rest upon our city."

But Odin sighed, and to himself he said, "O happy children, there shall yet come a day when darkness shall fall upon us; the Fenris-wolf shall again be loosed; and even the gods shall be no more."

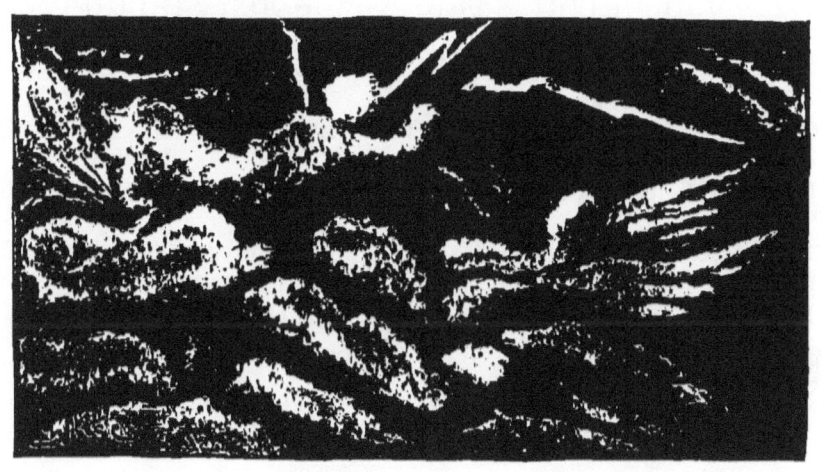

XVII.

DEFEAT OF HRUNGNER.

Greatest among the giants of Jotunheim, was Hrungner. Even the gods stood in fear of him; for when Thor's deep thunder rolled out across the skies, and the winds rose and the clouds grew black, it was Hrungner who, bold and defiant, shouted back with roars of scornful laughter — roars that rivalled in their thunder those of the great and mighty Thor.

"This giant," said the gods, standing in council together,—"this giant must be overcome. Too long have we suffered him to defy our power; too long have we borne his insolence; too long have his threats passed unnoticed by Odin the All-Father and by Thor the god of Thunder."

"I will go forth," said Odin, "upon my winged horse, my fleet-footed Sleipner, to meet this giant who dares defy the gods of Asgard."

Accordingly across the skies, over the sea to Jotunheim, rode Odin.

"It is a fine steed you ride, good stranger," bellowed Hrungner as Odin drew near; "almost as fine a steed as my own Goldfax, who can fly through the air and swim through the seas with the same ease that another steed might travel upon the plains of Midgard."

"But his speed cannot equal that of Sleipner," answered Odin quietly, his deep eyes burning with the light no giant could quite comprehend, and beneath which even Hrungner quailed at heart.

"Sleipner! Odin!" thundered Hrungner. "Are you Odin? And is this your Sleipner — the winged steed of which the gods of Asgard boast? Away with him! And I upon my Goldfax will prove to you that in Jotunheim lives one giant who dares challenge even Odin and his mighty war-horse to contest. Away! Away Odin! Away Sleipner! Away Hrungner! Away Goldfax!"

And with a shout that echoed even to the halls of Asgard, the great giant mounted his steed and soon brought him, neck to neck with Odin and his immortal Sleipner.

On, on, across the skies they flew.

Before their mighty force, the clouds scattered
hither and thither, striking against each other
with a crashing sound that to the earth-people
was like the voice of Thor.

From the eyes of the steeds the lightnings flashed; and from their reeking sides
the foam fell in showers upon the earth below.
The people, terror-stricken, ran to their caves
and prayed the gods to protect them from the
fury of the blast.

"It is like no storm we ever knew," they
whispered, one to the other. "The thunder!
the lightnings! the scurrying clouds! and with
it all, the roaring winds and the falling of
great white flakes, now like hail, now like
snow! Has Odin forgotten his children?
Have the Frost giants fallen upon Asgard?"
But now the storm was over. Odin and
Hrungner both had reached the walls of

Asgard. Through the great rolling gateway both had burst together; for the steed of the bold Hrungner had indeed proved himself equal to the snow-white Sleipner, whose magic powers no one but Odin fully knew.

Hrungner, elated with his success, and never once dreaming that, had Odin so willed it, he, with his brave steed Goldfax, might have been left far behind in the race, strode into the halls of Asgard and called loudly for food and drink and rest.

All these were granted him, and the giant threw himself down upon a golden couch and stared insolently upon the gods. All were there save Thor. "And where," bellowed Hrungner, "is the great god Thor, the mighty thunderer who dares defy the Frost giants; and whose strength is boasted greater than that of Hrungner, the chief of the mighty Frost giants?

"Bring him into my presence." roared the giant. "Let me prove to you that one giant at least dares defy even the greatest and most warlike of you all."

Away upon the sea, Thor heard this boast. "Who challenges me and defies my power?" he thundered; and with the swiftness of the wind, hastening upward toward the shining city, he burst in upon the giant stretched out upon the golden couch.

"I challenge you!" bellowed the giant, springing from his couch and facing the god of thunder.

Thor raised his hammer. The lightnings flashed from his eye. "Halt!" roared the giant. "Little credit will it be to the god of Thunder to fall in battle upon a Frost giant unarmed and unprotected. You are a coward! Fight me as becomes a great god on equal grounds and under fair conditions. Come to me in the land of Jotunheim, and there will I challenge you to battle. Then will your victory, if you win, lend lustre to your greatness; and the fear of you throughout the land of the Frost giants be greater than ever before." .

"As you say," answered Thor with a sneer. "Go now, and make ready for the holmgang,* in which the insolent, boastful Hrungner shall learn the power of the gods whom, in his ignorance, he dares defy."

Then Hrungner departed from the city of Asgard, and assembled the giants together to prepare for the coming battle. "Let us make a giant of clay," and at once every giant in Jotunheim fell to work. Whole mountains were leveled to the earth, and the great masses

---

* duel.

of stone and earth heaped high ; until, on the third day, there stood a giant nine miles high and three miles broad, ready to defy the power of the Thunder-god when he should come. But alas for the heart of this warrior of clay! None could be found, either in Midgard or in Jotunheim, of size proportionate to the body of the mighty creation ; and so, in despair, the heart of a sheep was chosen, and around it the clay warrior was built.

At the first sound of rolling thunder — by which the coming of Thor was announced afar off — alas ! this heart, fluttering and trembling, so shook the mighty form that its spear fell from its hand, its knees shook, and Hrungner was left to fight his battle alone with the angry son of Odin.

Onward, nearer and nearer, came Thor the Terrible. The lightnings flashed and the earth rumbled. Seizing a great mountain of flint in his hands, Hrungner waited. His eyes burned and his face was set.

Suddenly, forth from the ground beneath his feet, the god of Thunder burst. Hrungner sprang forward. With a mighty force he hurled the mountain of flint. Thor, with a roar, flung his mighty hammer. The two crashed together in midair. The flint broke, and one half of it was driven into the heavy skull of Thor. The hammer, cleaving the flint, sped onward, and Hrungner fell dead beneath its never-failing blow; but in falling his great body lay across the neck of Thor, who, stunned by the blow from the flint, had fallen, his hammer still clenched firmly in his powerful hand.

For a moment, there was a hush. The very sun stood still. Not a sound was heard

through Jotunheim. The thunder of battle
had died away; all the earth was still.

Then came Magne, a son of Thor.
"Why this sudden quiet?" he called. "Why
has my father's voice been stilled? Certainly
the great god Thor has not fallen in battle!"

"In the name of Odin," he thundered,
as he saw the Frost giant's body lying across
his father's massive frame,—"in the name of
Odin and of Thor, what does this mean?"
And, seizing the giant by a foot, he hurled
him out over the seas. For miles and miles
the giant's body cut the air, and then, falling, sank and was buried beneath the waves.

Thor staggered to his feet again, and
with a roar that made the leaves of Ygdrasil
tremble and shook even the halls of Valhalla,
set forth across the seas, never once looking
back towards the land of Jotunheim, whose

people for the time, at least, were again sub-
dued by the power of Thor, the god of
Thunder, — by Thor, the son of Odin the
All-wise.

XVIII.

THOR AND SKRYMER.

There was peace in all the lands; stilled were the Frost giants, and in Midgard all was happiness.

"Come with me, that I may see that you do no mischief," said Thor to Loke, as he sprang into his golden chariot, drawn by his snow-white goats.

All day the chariot wheeled on and on across the skies. Night fell, and the gods, entering a peasant's cottage, asked for shelter. "Our supper we have with us," Thor said. And taking the goats from the chariot, he killed them and placed them before the fire.

Never had the peasants taken part in such a feast. "It is a feast for the gods," they said; "but pray, how will you finish your journey without your goats?"

"We will attend to that," said Thor. "Eat what you will, and all you can. I only ask that, when the feast is finished, you promise to place all the bones together there before the door upon the goat skins. See to it that no bone is forgotten; and that not one — even the smallest — be lost or broken."

The peasants promised; the meat was eaten, and in due time the household went to bed and to sleep.

Morning came; and with the first flush

of light Thor arose, and, with his magic
hammer, sat down beside the heap of bones,
that lay upon the goat skins before the door.

"Kling! Kling! Kling!" sounded the
hammer, striking in turn each little bone; then
the two goats leaped forth, as white and
plump and round as ever, and as ready to spin
across the waters with the golden chariot of
their master.

But alas, one goat was lame. He held
up one tiny foot and moaned. "Some one of
you," roared Thor, "has broken a bone. Did
I not command that you be careful, and see
that every bone should be placed, uninjured,
upon the goat skins?"

The peasants shook with fear. They
knew now who this strange guest might be.
"It is Thor!" they whispered to each other.
"And that is the mighty hammer whose aim

never fails, and whose force is death to all upon whom it falls!"

"O thou great god Thor," cried the peasants, "spare us! Indeed had we known, not one bone would we have taken in our unhappy fingers; and all night long would we have watched beside the goat skins that no harm should come to them. Spare us, O spare us, great Thor! Take all we have — our house, our cattle, our children, everything — only spare our lives to us!"

Thor seized his hammer in his hand. His great knuckles grew white, so strong was his giant hold upon the handle. The peasants sank upon their knees. Their faces dropped and their eyes closed. Shaking with terror, they awaited the falling of the hammer.

"Up, up, ye peasants," thundered Thor. This offense I forgive. Your lives too, shall be spared you; but I will carry away with me these children of yours,—Thjalfe and Roskva; and they shall serve me in my journeys across the lands and over the seas."

"The goats I leave with you; and I charge you, by your lives see that no harm comes to them in any way. Come Thjalfe, come Roskva, place yourselves before the chariot, and bear me quickly across the seas."

All day long the chariot wheeled on and on, the children never tiring, until, at nightfall, they found themselves upon the shores of the country of the Frost giants.

Plunging into a deep forest, they hurried through and came out into a great plain beyond. Here they found a house, the very doors of which were as high as the mountains and as broad as the broadest river.

"We will rest here," said Thor, and,

spreading the great skins which they found near the doorway, they made for themselves beds, and soon were fast asleep.

At midnight they were awakened by a terrible roar. The whole house shook with its vibrations. Thor, seizing his hammer in his strong right hand, strode to the door. The whole earth trembled, but in the darkness even Thor could not see beyond the doorway.

Hour after hour he stood there, listening. Slowly, at last, the dawn began to come; the sun rose, and there, just at the edge of the forest, Thor saw the outstretched body of a giant, whose head was in itself a small mountain, and whose feet stretched away into the valley below.

"And it is you, then, that have rocked the very earth with your giant snores, and have taken from me my night of rest," thought

Thor, when he saw the giant form stretched out before him.

With one angry stride Thor reached the side of the sleeping giant. Raising his hammer a full mile into the air, he smote the giant full upon the skull, with a crash that sounded like the fall of a mighty oak.

"What is that?" asked the giant, opening his sleepy eyes. "Indeed, Thor, are you here? Something awoke me. I think an acorn must have dropped upon my head," said the giant, gathering himself to rise.

"Go to sleep again," growled Thor; "it isn't morning yet. I am going to sleep myself."

A few minutes and the snores of the giant rang through the air again.

"Now we will see," thought Thor. Again he crept to the giant's side. Lifting his hammer, this time two miles in the air, he brought it down upon the giant's skull with a crash that sounded like the breaking of the ice and the roaring of the torrent in a mighty river.

"What is that?" muttered the giant, only half awake. A leaf must have fallen upon my forehead. I will take myself out into the plain where I can sleep in peace."

"Go to sleep," answered Thor; "it is nearly morning, and will be time to wake up for the day before you reach the plain."

Again the giant fell asleep; and again the snoring rang out upon the air. "He shall not escape me this time," whispered Thor, creeping again to the giant's side. Raising his hammer, this time three miles in the air, he crashed it down upon the forehead of the giant with such force and fury that the very heavens reverberated; and the earth people,

springing frightened from their deep sleep,
called to each other, " The dwarfs are at their
forges! Did you not feel the earth shake and
the mountains tremble?"

"Well, well," droned the sleepy giant;
"the moss from the trees falls upon my face
and wakes me. It is nearly sunrise, and I may
as well arise and go on to Utgard. And you,
Thor,—I am told you, too, are journeying
towards the land of Utgard. But I must
hurry on. I will meet you there; but let me
give you warning that we are a race of giants
of no mean size. And great though you are,
it would be as well for you that you boast not
of your power among us. Even your mighty
hammer might fail to do its work among
giants of such strength and stature as those
of Skrymer's race."

There was a sneer on Skrymer's face as

he said this; but before Thor could raise his
hammer to punish him for his insolence, he
had crossed the great plain, and was already
miles away. Thor sat down beside the forest.
He was mortified, and vexed, and puzzled.
What did it mean? Had his hammer lost its
magic power? Was the giant Skrymer
immortal? He could not tell. There was a
heavy cloud upon his face as he set forth
again upon his journey. The little servants
shook with fear; even Loke kept silent, and
said not one word the live-long day.

A GIANT'S HOME.

XIX.

THOR AND THE UTGARD-KING.

Travelling on and on, through many days and many nights, Thor and his companions came to a great castle. Its pinnacles reached far up among the clouds, and its great gateways were broad even like the horizon itself.

In between the bars crept Thor and Loke and the children Thjalfe and Roska.

"Let us enter the castle," said Thor grimly. "It must be the palace of the king--

the Utgard-Loke — whose threats have defied
even the All-wisdom and the All-power of the
mighty Odin.

At these words the walls of the castle
trembled. The pillars of frost and the great
arches of ice glittered and glistened. Thjalfe
and Roska grew white with fear. "We hear
your voice," thundered Thor; "but we have
no fear of you even though you shake the
castle walls until they fall. And behold, we
dare come into your very presence, thou
terrible king of Utgard!"

The great king showed his glittering
teeth. His brow grew black with rage.

"This is Thor, the god of Thunder," he
sneered: "and so small are you that you can
creep through the bars of our gateway, pass
unnoticed by our sentinels, even into the very
presence of the king!"

Then Utgard-Loke — for this was the king's name — threw back his head and laughed until the whole earth shook; trees were uprooted, and avalanches of ice and snow, pouring down into valleys, buried hundreds of the little people of Midgard.

Thor clenched his hammer. He dared not thunder; even his lightnings were as nothing in this great palace hall and before the terrible voice of the Utgard-king.

" But perhaps you are greater than you look," continued the king, roaring again at his own wit. " Tell me what great feats you can accomplish; for no one is allowed entrance to this castle who cannot perform great deeds."

" I can perform great deeds — many of them," boasted Loke, nowise abashed, even in the presence of the terrible king. " I can eat faster than any creature in Midgard, in

Utgard, or even in Asgard, the home of the gods."

Again the king roared; and, placing before him a great wooden trough heaped high with food, he commanded his servant Loge to challenge Loke to the contest.

But alas for Loke, although the food disappeared before him like fields of grain beneath the scythe of steel, yet before the task was half begun, Loge had swallowed food, and trough, and all!

The king roared louder still; and Loke, never before beaten by giant power, shrank away, angry and threatening.

" But I," said Thjalfe, " can run. I can outrun any creature that lives on land or sea."

Then Thjalfe was placed beside a tiny little pigmy— Huge he was called; but hardly had they run a pace before Huge had shot so far ahead that Thjalfe, crestfallen, went and hid himself behind the great ice pillar that stood outside the castle gate.

And now Thor rose to his feet and drew himself up to his greatest height; but even that seemed as nothing compared with the enormous stature of the Utgard-king. He clenched the hammer tightly and thundered as never he had thundered before. The tiny fringe of icicles trembled. Then Utgard-Loke laughed; and with his thunder the whole castle rocked and reeled.

"And will Thor contest with the power of Utgard?" asked the king. "I will," roared Thor, and there was a fire in his eye that even Utgard shrank before.

But Utgard only roared in turn and brought to Thor a great horn, filled to its brim with sparkling water.

"Drink," said he; "and if one half the power is yours that Odin claims, you will empty the horn at a single draught."

Thor seized the horn. One long, deep draught, such as no mortal, no giant, nor even another god could have drawn — and the horn was hardly one drop less full.

The king roared till the icicles and the fringes of frost, swaying and rocking beneath the thunder, fell with a crash upon the palace floor.

"Can the great god Thor boast no greater power than that? Once more, thou greatest of all the sons of Odin — once more lift the horn in thy mighty hands and show us the greatness of the gods of Asgard."

Thor, stung by the sneer of the Utgard-king, raised the horn again to his lips; and calling upon the name of Odin and all the

gods of the shining city, drank again. Higher
and higher he raised the horn, deeper and
deeper drew he the draught. But alas, again,
when the horn was lowered, the waters were
no lower than before.

"You seem not so great as we the frost
giants have believed," said the king with a
cold sneer.

Thor's anger rose. His blood boiled
with rage and fury. With a burst of thunder
and a flash of lightning that shattered the
pillars of the great hall, he seized the horn
again. Three long hours passed. Utgard-
Loke trembled with fear and dread; for never
for one second had the angry god taken the
horn from his lips. "The ruin of the Utgard
kingdom is come," he groaned. "There is no
hope for victory over such a god. The horn
— even the magic horn — will fail before the

might of this fierce and awful Thor, the god
of Thunder."

Then Thor lifted the horn from his lips.
Defiance flashed from his eye. The king of
the Frost giants trembled. Both looked into
the horn. Alas for Thor! Even now hardly
could it be counted one quarter emptied.
Darkness gathered over the strong god's face.
Courage sprang into the eyes of the king.
"Let not your valor fail you," said the king,
taking the horn from the hand of Thor. "You
are great — you have proved it, in that you
have, even in so small a degree as this,
emptied the horn from which none but a god
could have quaffed one drop. It is only that
your greatness is less than you have boasted,
and less than we have believed it to be."

"I will not stand defeated," thundered
Thor. "Bring before me another challenge.

I will not go forth until the giants of Utgard have indeed known and felt the power of Thor, the god whose lightnings rend the skies, and whose thunders rock the very mountains of the earth."

"Once more, then, shall you contend for power," said the Utgard-king. "And this time with Elle, the toothless giant of endless years, before whose power bend all the strongest sons of Midgard, and before whom, in some far off day, even the gods of Asgard shall bow as powerless as the children of Midgard."

Thor sprang upon the giant Elle. Like a demon of the under world he fought, and for a time even this All-conquering giant swayed before the wild madness of his bursts of thunder, and his crashing, hissing bolts of fire. But alas for Thor! Even his godlike strength was doomed to fail him. He trembled; his sight vanished; a strange chill settled over him, and he sank, conquered, before the power of the giant Elle.

And now the night had fallen upon the land. The light had faded from the mountain tops; and the chill of night was in the frosty air. Exhausted, the great god wrapped him-self about and sank into heavy sleep. And his dreams were of great battles, of terrible foes, and of the last great day which, sometime in the ages to come, should fall upon the city of the gods, and in which even the power of Odin should fail, and the light go out from all the earth. All night long these dreams haunted the great heart of Thor; and in the morning the people in Midgard said, "It was a strange night. Through all the hours of darkness, the thunders rolled in the distance, and the pale lightnings flashed among the mountain peaks beyond the seas."

In the morning, even with the first rays of light, Thor, with Loke and Thjalfe and Roskva, set forth upon their journey homeward. There was a terrible blackness upon the face of Thor, and the thunders rumbled deeply. Never before had Thor known the bitterness of defeat, and he returned to Asgard and to Odin sick at heart.

, "Lose not thy courage, Thor," said the All-wise. "Know that thou art not even now defeated in any test of true strength. Utgard-Loke has triumphed to be sure; but even he trembles now, and has closed the doors of his castle, and has set thousands upon thousands of sentinels to watch against thy return.

The horn from which thou didst drink reached far down into the depths of the sea;

and the people of Midgard even now throng the shores and wonder what power in heaven or in earth can so have shrunken the great waters of the sea.

Loge, with whom Loke contended, was none less than Wild Fire; and Huge was Thought itself. Even the gods, even Odin himself, with these would but contend in vain. And Elle — it is indeed as Utgard-Loke said — no power in heaven itself can equal hers. She is the all-powerful, the never-failing, the ever-present Old Age. All the people of the earth, all the gods of Asgard — aye, even the Earth and Asgard must one day fall before her mighty will. That you contended even as you did, has driven terror deep into the hearts of the cruel Frost giants; nor do they doubt that you are the terrible god of Thunder, the greatest of all the sons of Odin."

XX.

THOR AND THE MIDGARD SERPENT.

With these words of Odin, Thor's courage rose. "Bring me my hammer," he called to Sif, "and again will I go forth into the realms of the Frost giants."

The great Odin smiled. "Fear not, my son. Remember there can be no defeat to Thor, the son of Odin, whose mighty hand holds firm the terrible hammer forged by the dwarfs of the under world."

Then Thor sprang into his chariot. "Away, away," he thundered, "to the home of Hymer—the hateful, boastful Hymer! Away to the land of the Frost giants! Once, and for all, Thor will prove to them the power and the terror of the gods of Asgard."

The wheels of the chariot rumbled and rolled. From their spokes the lightnings flashed. With the speed of Thought itself, it hissed and whistled through the air. The clouds, scattering, raised a mighty wind.

In Midgard the leaves ran like fire before the gale; the trees rocked; and ever and anon the moaning wind rose and fell like the voice of a mighty tempest.

"It is the Valkyries!" the people of Midgard said. "Always does the wind rise; always do the clouds hurry across the skies when the Valkyries set forth to battle. Somewhere there is war in our fair earth; somewhere heroes are falling on the bloody battlefield."

For, in all this time, there had come to be many people in Midgard. The children of Ask and Embla had become men and women, had grown old, and their children, too, had become men and women.

And there were wars in the land. Warriors in the east fought those in the west; those in the north fought those in the south.

But the warriors were brave men; and over every battle Odin watched, grinding the spears, now shielding and protecting, now forcing the warriors into the very hottest of the battle. And when the battle was over, and all was quiet, when the great sun had sunk behind the hills of Jotunheim, and the soft moon shone down upon the battle-field, then Odin would call to the Valkyries,

and bid them go down into Midgard and
bring with them to Valhalla all who had
fallen bravely fighting. For this was the
hero's reward. With this hope he entered
battle; with this hope he fought; with this
hope he turned his dying eyes towards Mt.
Ida and thanked the All-father that now he,
too, might enter into the joys of Asgard and
know the glory of immortal life in the golden
halls of Valhalla.

And now the winds had died away; the
clouds were at rest; there was peace over
Midgard. For the chariot had reached the
home of the Frost giants, and Thor had
entered the great rock-bound castle of the
giant Hymer.

"Let us go out upon the sea to fish," said
Thor to the dread giant, with whom he longed
to measure power.

Seizing the oars, Thor himself rowed the great boat out into the sea. "Give me the oars," bellowed Hymer; "you have already rowed a long way and must be wearied."

"I wearied!" thundered Thor. "Indeed I have not rowed one half the distance. I shall row even into the realm of the Midgard Serpent, whose length lies coiled round about Midgard, and whose home is deep down beneath the raging waters. There only shall we find fish worthy of the bait of a god."

Hymer trembled. He feared the Midgard Serpent, whose great coils so lashed the waters of the ocean that they rose, white with foam, even to the very mountain tops. "The fishing just here has never failed. There is no need to row farther into the ocean," said Hymer, hoping to dissuade the god from rowing farther from the shores of Jotunheim.

"But I must fish in mid-ocean, and in the deepest of the waters," was Thor's reply.

For hours and hours they rowed. The mountain tops grew dimmer and dimmer in the blue distance; no land could be seen; the waters sparkled and shone on every side as far as the eye could reach.

"We will make this our fishing place," said Thor, at last, throwing down his oars and preparing the great cable that should serve him for a line. This he gave into the hands of the trembling giant, and prepared for himself another. The hours passed, but no fish had been drawn into the boat.

"Had you listened to me," thundered Hymer, "our boat might long before this have been filled with the fish I have never failed to catch in waters nearer the shores of the land of the Frost giants."

"Do you think a god would be content with less than the greatest fish in all the sea?" thundered Thor. "Do you not know I shall bring to this boat's edge the terrible Midgard Serpent itself?"

And even as he spoke he gathered in his line, and dashed upon the boat floor a whale of such enormous size that even the giant looked with amazement upon so terrible a display of the fisherman's strength and power. Surely this must be Thor himself!

"The whale is yours," muttered Thor, unfastening his line and throwing it overboard again. "I have no care for fish as small as this."

Suddenly there was a rush of waters. It was as if a terrible tempest had burst upon the sea. The waters seethed and foamed. The great waves rose mountain high. The boat rocked and reeled, and the green waters, pouring over its sides, filled it so that the great whale floated out upon the sea.

"It is the Midgard Serpent!" roared Thor; and his mighty voice, rising even above the rush of the great sea, mingled with the thunder of the breaking waves and echoed out to the shores of the farthest lands.

Thor sprang from the boat and planted himself firmly upon the great rocks beneath the sea. The giant, dumb with terror, clung to the sides of the rocking boat. On, on came the serpent, nearer and nearer, the roaring waves and the heaping foam bursting closer and closer upon the mountain-like boat that tossed now like seaweed upon the angry waters.

One burst like thunder, and the terrible serpent's head rose above the foam and glistened in the light. Thor sprang forward; and, with his mighty arm, threw the cable about the slimy neck of the Midgard Serpent and dragged him to the boat's edge. The giant sprang to his feet.

"Give me my hammer!" thundered the god.

"I will not!" thundered the giant; and with one quick bound he sprang forward, raised his shining sword, and with a sweep miles high, cut the great cable which held the writhing serpent.

Another roar, and the great serpent arched his back even to the blue dome of the sky above. Then, with a hiss that sounded through Midgard and even up to the shining city of the fair Mt. Ida, he shot down beneath the waters, and over him closed the angry waves.

The foam dashed mountains high; the caves howled and boomed; the skies echoed crash on crash; and the whole earth trembled with the upheaval of the troubled waters. A rushing back, a heaping up, a breaking of great waves — and never again, by man or giant or god, was the loathsome serpent seen above the waters, until on that last sad, fateful day when the light had gone out from the sun, and the dread chill of Ragnarok had fallen even upon Valhalla and the beautiful shining city of Asgard.

A NORSE GALLEY.

VALKYRIES' SONG.

The Sea-king looked o'er the brooding wave;
   He turned to the dusky shore,
And there seemed, through the arch of a tide-worn cave
   A gleam, as of snow, to pour;
     And forth, in watery light,
     Moved phantoms, dimly white,
   Which the garb of woman bore.

Slowly they moved to the billow side;
   And the forms, as they grew more clear,
Seemed each on a tall, pale steed to ride,
   And a shadowy crest to rear,

And to beckon with faint hand,
From the dark and rocky strand,
And to point a gleaming spear.

Then a stillness on his spirit fell,
Before th' unearthly train,
For he knew Valhalla's daughters well,
The Choosers of the slain !
And a sudden rising breeze
Bore, across the moaning seas,
To his ear their thrilling strain.
* * * * *
" Regner ! tell thy fair-haired bride
She must slumber at thy side !
Tell the brother of thy breast,
Even for him thy grave hath rest !
Tell the raven steed which bore thee,
When the wild wolf fled before thee,
He too with his lord must fall,—
There is room in Odin's Hall ! "
* * * * *
There was arming heard on land and wave,
When afar the sunlight spread,
And the phantom forms of the tide-worn cave
With the mists of morning fled ;
But at eve, the kingly hand
Of the battle-axe and brand,
Lay cold on a pile of dead ! — *Hemans.*

XXI.

THE DYING BALDUR.

Ages upon ages had rolled away. And now the day of sorrow, which always Odin had known must come, drew near.

Already the god of song had gone with his beautiful wife Idun down into the dark valley of death; and there was a new strange rustle among the leaves of Ygdrasil, like the rustling of leaves that were dead.

Odin's face grew sad; and, try as he would, he could not join with the happy gods about him in their joys and festal games.

"Odin," said Frigg one day, "tell me what grieves thee; what weighs thee down and puts such sadness into thine eyes and heart."

" Baldur himself shall tell you all," answered Odin sadly.

Then Baldur seated himself in the midst of the gods and said: " Always, since Odin drank at the Well of Wisdom, and learned the secrets of the past and of the future, has he known that a time would come when the light must go out from Baldur's eyes; and he, although a god, must go down into the dark valley. Now that time draws near. Already have Brage and Idun gone from us; and with them have gone song and youth. Soon will Baldur go, and with him must go the light and warmth he has always been so glad to bring to Asgard and to Midgard both."

"O Baldur! Baldur! Baldur! My child! my child! my child!" cried Frigg. "This cannot be! this shall not be! I will go down from Asgard. I will go up and down the earth, and every rock and tree and plant shall pledge themselves to do no harm to thee."

"Dear mother Frigg," sighed Baldur, "you cannot change what is foretold. From the beginning of time this was decreed, that one day the light should go out from heaven and the twilight of the gods should fall."

There was a long silence in the hall of Asgard. No god had courage to speak. Their hearts were heavy, and they had no wish to speak.

The sun sank behind the western hills. Its rich sunset glow spread over the golden city and over the beautiful earth below. Then darkness followed slowly, slowly creeping,

creeping on, up the mountain side, across the summit, until even the shining city stood dark and shadowy beneath the gathering twilight.

"Like this, some day, the twilight will fall upon our city," said Odin; "and it will never, never rise again."

The mother heart of Frigg would not accept even Odin's word. And when the sun's first rays shot up above the far-off hills, Frigg stole forth from Asgard down the rainbow bridge to Midgard.

To every lake, and river, and sea, she hurried, and said: "Promise me, O waters, that Baldur's light shall never go out because of you."

"We promise," the waters answered. And Frigg hurried on to the metals. "Promise me, O metals, that Baldur's light shall never go out because of you."

"We promise," answered the metals. And Frigg hurried on to the minerals. "Promise me, O minerals," she said, "that Baldur's light shall never go out because of you."

"We promise," answered the minerals. And Frigg hurried on to the fire, the earth, the stones, the trees, the shrubs, the grasses, the birds, the beasts, the reptiles; and even to the abode of pale disease she went. Of each she asked the same earnest, anxious question; and from each she received the same kind, honest answer.

As the sun sank behind the high peaks of the Frost giants' homes, Frigg, radiant and happy, her eyes bright and her heart alive with hope, sped up the rainbow bridge. Triumphant, she hurried into the great hall to Odin and Baldur.

"Be happy again, O Odin! Be happy again, O Baldur! There is no danger, no sorrow to come to us from anything in the earth or under the earth. For every tree has promised me; and every rock and every metal; every animal and every bird. Even the waters and the fire have promised that never harm through them shall come to Baldur."

But, alas, for poor Frigg. One little

weed, a wee little weed, hidden beneath a rock, she had overlooked. Loke, who had followed closely upon her in all her wanderings through the day, had not failed to notice this oversight of Frigg's. His wicked face shone with glee. His eyes gleamed; and as the radiant Frigg sped up the rainbow bridge, he hurried away to his home among the Frost giants to tell them of the little weed which, by and by, should work such harm to Baldur, in shutting out his life and light from Asgard and the earth.

The ages rolled on. Every one in Asgard, save Odin, had long ago thrown off the shadow of fear. "No harm can come to Baldur," they would say; and all save Odin believed it.

But a day came when Odin, looking down into the home of the dead, saw there the spirits moving about, hastening hither and thither.

"Something is happening there in the pale valley," said Odin. "They are preparing for the coming of another shade. And it must be some great one who is to come. See how great the preparation is they make."

"We prepare for the coming of Baldur," answered the shades as Odin came upon them, busy in their work. "We prepare a throne for Baldur. We prepare a throne for Baldur."

"For Baldur?" asked Odin, his heart sinking. "For Baldur!" chanted the shades. "For Baldur! Baldur cometh! Baldur cometh!"

And Odin, his godlike heart faint and sick at the thought, turned away and went slowly up the rainbow bridge.

There, in the great garden of the gods, he found Thor and Baldur and their brother

Hodor playing at tests of strength. Behind Hodor, invisible, stood Loke. In his hand he held a spear.

"Shame upon you, Hodor," whispered Loke, "that you, the strong and mighty Hodor, cannot overcome Baldur in a test of strength. Baldur may be beautiful and sunny, and he is a great joy to the world; that we know. But what is he compared with Hodor for strength?"

"But the spears will not touch him.. See how they glance away. Indeed it is true: Light cannot be pierced." answered Hodor, good-naturedly.

"Take this spear," said Loke, quietly. "It is less clumsy than those you throw."

Hodor took it, never thinking of any harm. Alas for Baldur and Asgard and all the happy smiling Earth! It was a spear tipped with the mistletoe —— the one plant that

BALDUR, THE BEAUTIFUL, IS DEAD.

Frigg had failed to find. The one plant that had not promised to do no harm to Baldur.

Quickly the spear flew through the air. One second, and Baldur the Summer Spirit, Baldur the Light of the Earth fell — dead.

"O, Asgard! Baldur is dead!" groaned Odin. "O Asgard, Asgard! Baldur is dead!"

Hodor, Thor, the gods, one and all, stood pale and white. A terrible fear settled over their faces. They shook with terror.

And even as they stood there, speechless in their grief, a twilight dimness began to fall lightly, lightly over all. The shining pavements grew less bright; the blue of the great arch overhead deepened; and in the valleys of Midgard there were long black shadows. Baldur was dead. The light had failed. The golden age was at an end. Now, even the gods must die.

XXII.

THE PUNISHMENT OF LOKE.

" It is Loke that has done this!" thundered Thor, seizing the great hammer in his clenched fists. " Nor will the gods of Asgard forgive this crime. No promise of his, no begging, no pleading shall save him from the punishment that belongs to him.

" O Baldur, Baldur! That I had slain the evil Loke ages upon ages ago — when he stole the hair from the glorious Sif; when he stole the necklace from the beautiful Freyja; when he carried Idun and the Apples of Life away into the home of the Frost giants; when he stung the dwarf and broke short the handle of my mighty hammer. Had I slain him then, this sorrow need not have come to us. O Baldur, Baldur!"

And the whole earth shook with the grief of Thor. The skies grew black. The wind shrieked. The lightnings flashed across the sky. His tears fell in torrents down the mountain sides; trees were swept away, and the swollen rivers rushed and roared along their course.

Never, even in the memory of the gaunt old giant at the Well of Wisdom, had such a storm of wind and rain and thunder and lightning been known. The earth-people fled to the mountain caves in terror.

"It is the wrath of Thor!" cried Loke, gasping with dread. "Let me hide myself till it is over." And changing himself into a fish, he dived deep into the great seething mass of angry waters.

But Thor and Odin were close upon him. The fiery eye of Thor had caught the sparkle of its shiny coat as the great fish shot down from the mountain side into the sea. Then, too, of what use was it to hide from the great, all-seeing eye of Odin? Did he not see and hear all sights and sounds? And, more than that, did he not know all things even from the beginning?

"We will take a great net, and we will drag the sea," said Odin quietly.

Loke heard these words and trembled. He hid himself beneath the sea-weed; but so muddy were the waters that he was driven out to breathe. The great net was spread. Held by the hands of Odin and of Thor, there was no escape for Loke. Sullenly he allowed the net to close over him. There was no other way; for it stretched from shore to shore and from above the waters even to the ocean bed.

And so, at last, because it was to be, the fish held; and Loke was in the power of the angry Thor.

"Come back," commanded Odin, "to your own shape and size." Loke obeyed; and in his own form was borne to Asgard. The angry gods fell, one and all, upon him. Not one showed pity for him. They hated him. And well they might; for had he not slain Baldur, and so loosed the power of the Frost giants upon their shining city.

"Let him be bound! Let him be bound!" they cried.

LOKE IN CHAINS.
From an Ancient Scandinavian Stone.

"Let him be bound even as the Fenris-wolf is bound!"

"Let him be bound with iron fetters!"

" Let him be nailed to the great rocks in the sea ! "

" Let a poisonous serpent hang over him ; and let the serpent drop, moment by moment, through all the time to come, his burning poison upon him ! Let him lie there, chained and suffering till the last great day ! "

"All this shall be," thundered Thor. And thus it was that the cruel, evil-hearted, peace-destroyer Loke, suffered ages upon ages of punishment for his malice and his crime.

THE NORNS.

XXIII.

THE DARKNESS THAT FELL ON ASGARD.

The gods had avenged themselves upon the cruel Peace-destroyer, and he lay suffering the tortures they had put upon him.

But even this could not bring back the sunny god, the happy, cheerful, life-giving Baldur. Brage had gone, and there was no sound of music in Asgard; Idun had gone, and signs of age were again creeping over the faces of the gods; now Baldur was gone, and with him the long light and warm softness of the summer time.

"He may come back," Frigg would say; and every morning she strained her eyes to see if he had risen from behind the far-off hills with the soft light she had learned to know so well. "Baldur is late," she would say, as the days rolled on.

But all this time, from the cold north land, the Frost giants, triumphant, were drawing near. Their chill breath was in the air. The days grew short; the nights grew long. The rivers were locked in ice. Great drifts of snow were everywhere. The sky was gray; and there were no stars. The sun shone pale and white through the dull clouds and the blinding drifts of snow. It grew bitter, bitter cold.

"The Fimbul-winter!" whispered the earth-people. "Has the Fimbul-winter come?" And Odin answered, "Yes; it is true. The Fimbul-winter, foretold by the Norns, even from the beginning of time, has come. Soon the great wolf will spring forth from the under world, and he will seize upon the sun and devour it. Then dense darkness will fall upon us; and Ragnarok — the end of all things — will be upon us."

And it came to pass as Odin said. One day there was heard a mighty rumbling. This time it was not the thunder from the mighty hammer of great Thor. His hands were frozen; nor had he heart to try to wield his hammer.

The thunder and the rumble came this time from within the earth. The great earth trembled and shook. Great gaping mouths

opened and swallowed up the children; the
mountains crumbled and fell; the great
serpent lashed the sea; the great rocks rocked
and swayed and tore themselves apart. Loke
and the Fenris-wolf, freed from their fetters,
sprang forth, burning with hate and wild for
vengeance. The Frost giants already were
upon the rainbow bridge. A terrible battle
followed.

The gods fell, one by one: Thor by the
deadly flood of poison from the Midgard
serpent; Tyre in the great jaws of the Fenris-
wolf, who, ages before, had torn from him his
strong right hand.

And now the battle was over. The gods
lay dead — even Odin. The shining city of
Asgard was a blackened, smoking ruin; the
rainbow bridge was gone. The giants sent
forth their cold winds, howling with cruel glee.

Loke's evil heart was glad; the great serpent lashed the waters mountain high; and the earth-people perished in the flood. The Fenris-wolf stretched its great jaw from heaven to earth and shook the skies.

There was a strange hush! A great ball of fire had fallen upon the battle field. There was a sudden rush of air! A great wave of heat spread out across all space! A burst of thunder! A crackling as of fire! Then one hiss, and the whole earth was one great scorching blaze.

One second— a fierce red tongue of flame had shot up the trunk of Ygdrasil, and it fell, a mass of blackened ashes. The sea hissed and steamed. The earth melted. The Frost giants, Loke, the serpent, the Fenris-wolf, all, all were wrapped in flame. A second more, and there was no living thing in all the earth.

For Ragnarok, the Reign of Fire, had come;
and with it came an end to Life — and end
alike to gods and giants; an end to all
creatures of the land and sea; an end even to
the great earth itself.

VOCABULARY.

As'gard : (*s* like *z*) Abode of the gods.

Ask : The first woman ; made from a tree.

Baldur : (Bäl'-dur) The god of summer sunshine.

Bauge : (Boúgh-ge : hard *g*) A giant brother of Suttung.

Brá-ge : (*a* as in *far:* hard *ge*) A son of Odin and famed for **wisdom** and eloquence.

Brok : (pronounced Brock) A dwarf.

Bölverk : (*o* like *e* in heard, Bél-verk) A name assumed by Odin.

Elle : Old age.

Embla : The first man ; made from a tree.

Fenris wolf : Monster wolf, son of Loki.

Frigg : Wife of Odin.

Frey : (Fray) Ruler over the light elves.

Frey-ja : (*e* as in *let*, *j* like *y*, Fréy-ya) Sister of Frey ; half the fallen in battle belonged to her.

Fimbul : The terrible winter just before the destruction of the earth.

Gold-fax : Hrungner's horse.

Huge : (Hoó-ge : hard *g*) Thought.

Hödor : (*o* as *e* in heard, Hö'-der) The slayer of Baldur.

Hrung-ner : (Hroon'-gner) A giant.

Hy′-mer : A giant, owner of the kettle, Mile-deep.

Idun : (Īdoon) Keeper of the Apples of Youth.

I-fing : Name of a river.

Jötunheim : (j like y, o like e in heard : Yér-toon-heém) Home of the giants.

Loke, or Loki : (Lō-kĕ) The evil giant god.

Loge : (Lō-gē : hard g) Wild-fire.

Mid-gard : The abode of men.

Magne : (Mág-ne) Thor's son.

Norn : (Nórn) The Three . fates represented as three young women.

Njord : (often spelled Ni-örd pronounced Nee-yèrd) Father of Frey and Freyja.

Odin : (ŏ-din) The fountain head of wisdom.

Ragnarök : (rag′-na-rék) Twilight of the gods.

Roskva : (rósk-va) A peasant girl who went with Thor to Utgard Loki's.

Sindre, or Sindri : (sín-dre) A dwarf.

Sif : (Seef) Thor's wife.

Suttung : (supposed to be derived from Sup-tung) The giant who obtained the precious wine.

Sleip-ner : Odin's horse.

Skry-mer : (Skry-mer) The giant who met Thor in the forest.

Thjal-fe: (Thy'al-fe) A peasant boy who went with Thor to Utgard Loki's.

Thrym: A giant who stole Thor's hammer.

Thor: Thunder-god.

Utgard: The abode of Loki.

Valhalla: (val-hál-la) The hall to which Odin took those slain in battle.

Valkyrie: (Val-ky'-rie) Handmaidens of Odin.

Vafthrudnur: (Vaf-thród-neer) A giant visited by Odin.

Ygdrasil: (íg-dras-il) The world-embracing ash tree.